"David Rosenfelt has written an excellent first entry to his second series. . . . It's told in a fresh voice by a sympathetic protagonist who will draw you into the book and keep you engrossed until the end."   —Marilyn's Mystery Reads

"[An] engaging series launch."   —*Stop, You're Killing Me!*

ALSO BY DAVID ROSENFELT

ANDY CARPENTER NOVELS

Best in Snow

Dog Eat Dog

Silent Bite

Muzzled

Dachshund Through the Snow

Bark of Night

Deck the Hounds

Rescued

Collared

The Twelve Dogs of Christmas

Outfoxed

Who Let the Dog Out?

Hounded

Unleashed

Leader of the Pack

One Dog Night

Dog Tags

New Tricks

Play Dead

Dead Center

Sudden Death

Bury the Lead

First Degree

Open and Shut

K TEAM NOVELS

The K Team

THRILLERS

Black and Blue

Fade to Black

Blackout

Without Warning

Airtight

Heart of a Killer

On Borrowed Time

Down to the Wire

Don't Tell a Soul

NONFICTION

Lessons from Tara: Life Advice from the World's Most Brilliant
Dog

Dogtripping: 25 Rescues, 11 Volunteers, and 3 RVs on Our Canine
Cross-Country Adventure

Praise for David Rosenfelt

"[Rosenfelt] has been more than one kind of writer in his life and never fails to deliver full value."   —*Sullivan County Democrat*

"Rosenfelt, like Dick Francis, keeps coming up with inventive ways to ensnare his hero in cases involving animals."

—*Kirkus Reviews*

"David Rosenfelt never disappoints!"   —*Fresh Fiction*

Praise for *Animal Instinct*

"A solid follow-up to [*The K Team*]."   —Red Carpet Crash

"Artfully spun."   —*BookPage*

"A second outing for Paterson's preeminent investigators ensnares one of their own members in uncomfortable ways. . . . Though the case is a hot mess, the criminals' sublimely simple central concept is worth all those subsidiary homicides."   —*Kirkus Reviews*

"Rosenfelt smoothly mixes humor with a sharp plot and appealing characters. This series deserves a long run."   —*Publishers Weekly*

"[*Animal Instinct*] kept my interest well into the night. I highly recommend this new series."   —*Deadly Pleasures*

"David Rosenfelt is the funniest man on the planet writing about murders. . . . A chiller with laughs."

—David Rothenberg on WBAI Radio

"Nicely done." —ReviewingtheEvidence.com

"If you love mysteries, sarcasm, and dogs, not necessarily in that order, you'll love Rosenfelt's books."
—*Kings River Life Magazine*

Praise for *The K Team*

"*The K Team* makes a strong companion to Rosenfelt's ongoing series, and it should be fighting crime for many novels."
—Associated Press

"Fans of the Andy Carpenter series will find much to enjoy here, including some cameos from Carpenter himself."
—*Library Journal*

"This strong series launch . . . is a promising start to what's likely to be a long-running series." —*Publishers Weekly*

"Corey serves as an investigator and narrator every bit as ebullient as Andy and a lot more diligent. . . . If you liked Rosenfelt's rollicking previous series, you'll like this one too."
—*Kirkus Reviews*

"David Rosenfelt is a master of the mystery/suspense genre, and with *The K Team* he has launched a new and inherently entertaining series." —*Midwest Book Review*

"I'm happy as a clam to keep reading the Andy Carpenter books and now have the K Team books to add to my reading enjoyment. Highly recommended." —*Deadly Pleasures*

ANIMAL INSTINCT

D A V I D   R O S E N F E L T

MINOTAUR
BOOKS
NEW YORK

For Riley and Oliver

Published in the United States by Minotaur Books, an imprint of St. Martin's Publishing Group

ANIMAL INSTINCT. Copyright © 2021 by Tara Productions, Inc. All rights reserved. Printed in the United States of America. For information, address St. Martin's Publishing Group, 120 Broadway, New York, NY 10271.

www.minotaurbooks.com

Designed by Omar Chapa

The Library of Congress has cataloged the hardcover edition as follows:

Names: Rosenfelt, David, author.
Title: Animal instinct / David Rosenfelt.
Description: First edition. | New York : Minotaur Books, 2021. |
    Series: K team novels ; 2
Identifiers: LCCN 2020048550 | ISBN 9781250257208 (hardcover) |
    ISBN 9781250257215 (ebook)
Subjects: GSAFD: Mystery fiction.
Classification: LCC PS3618.O838 A83 2021 | DDC 813/.6—dc23
LC record available at https://lccn.loc.gov/2020048550

ISBN 978-1-250-82942-9 (trade paperback)

Our books may be purchased in bulk for promotional, educational, or business use. Please contact your local bookseller or the Macmillan Corporate and Premium Sales Department at 1-800-221-7945, extension 5442, or by email at MacmillanSpecialMarkets@macmillan.com.

First Minotaur Books Trade Paperback Edition: 2022

D   10 9 8 7 6 5 4 3 2

LISA Yates was trying to live normally.

That's what she was telling herself, although the truth was that she was merely trying to appear as if nothing was wrong. That was not easy to do, because something was very wrong, and there was no longer anything normal about her life.

Lisa Yates was terrified.

She had been living with that fear for a long time. She finally decided that she would face it directly, but doing so was an extraordinarily risky proposition. This was not necessarily an act of courage, because she believed, knew in her soul, that not doing anything was even more dangerous.

The other thing she knew was that success depended on no one suspecting what she was planning. She was afraid to do it alone; something like going to the police or FBI scared her. She had decided she needed a lawyer, but did not know who to approach. And she had to be extraordinarily careful in whatever she did.

They could well be watching.

So this was intended to seem to be a normal evening out. She had no desire to go out; her inclination was to stay at home, obsess about her situation, and go over her plan for the thousandth time. Instead she'd spend a couple of hours making small talk, more for show than to help her forget her dilemma. Nothing could get her to forget.

So she went out to dinner with Una Loge, a former colleague at work who had left when she got married. Lisa had stayed fairly close with Una and her husband, Dave, but Lisa's own domestic situation by its very nature kept them somewhat apart. Lisa's domestic situation, at least until a month ago, was a train wreck.

They went to Manero's, in Teaneck. While pretending to be attentive and in the moment, Lisa let Una do most of the talking. But while Lisa was physically present, her mind was a million miles away.

The dinner took a little over two hours. Lisa revealed nothing about herself, not even sharing stories about the office, though Una still knew most of the people there. Una could tell that something was wrong and inquired about it, but when Lisa said that everything was fine, Una backed off. She wanted to give her friend space but was clearly worried for her.

Lisa quickly grabbed the check when it arrived, more in desperation to end the dinner than to show generosity. She had to get out of there, her mind was exploding, and she couldn't pretend anymore. She told Una that she could pay next time, though Lisa doubted there would be a next time.

They said good night at the restaurant's front door and Lisa walked to her car on the street, not more than fifty feet away, while Una stayed behind, having used valet parking.

Lisa had just reached her car when she heard the noise. In

that split second, she knew what was happening, but she did not have time to react, and she did not feel the bullet pierce her skull.

She would never be afraid again.

I am staring fear in the face; it is coming at me in waves.

I don't mean that as a metaphor; the waves are literally coming at me . . . one after another, in varying sizes and strengths.

I am standing at the water's edge of the Eighth Avenue Dog Beach in Asbury Park, New Jersey. I rarely came to Asbury Park as a kid; in those days it was in decline and disrepair. I never understood how that could happen to a city with such a large and beautiful beach; it would seem to be a prime real estate location and immune to such a fate.

But the municipal decay was an unfortunate fact, so for our vacations, the Douglas family always went a bit farther south, to Long Beach Island. Since then Asbury has made a remarkable comeback and is now a thriving community . . . and the dog beach is cool.

So here I am.

With me at the moment are Dani Kendall, who I can no longer

deny is my serious girlfriend, and Simon Garfunkel, my longtime pal and partner. Simon is a German shepherd and functioned as my K-9 comrade on the Paterson police force for almost eight years, before our recent simultaneous retirement.

My earliest fear in life was as a result of my first trip to the beach. I was with my mother and brother, and we were staying in a boardinghouse on Long Beach Island. We used to go there for a two-week vacation every summer, but my father would come down only on weekends. He was a sergeant in the Paterson PD, and he worked overtime as much as he could. I can never remember him taking a weekday off. Even taking Saturday and Sunday during our vacation was a major concession on his part.

I was probably four years old and excited to be going in the ocean for the first time. Then my mother killed that feeling of anticipation by warning me of the undertow, or riptide, or whatever she called it. It was an invisible, mysterious force in the water capable of dragging small children off to certain, horrible death. And, according to her, it was relentless and overpowering; once a child was in its grip, it was over.

So the four-year-old Corey Douglas did not go in the ocean that day, or any day since. Literally never; I've always considered the downside to be too great.

It's not a phobia. The dictionary defines phobia as an inexplicable or irrational fear. That doesn't apply here; it's very rational to be afraid of being dragged to one's death by the ocean monster known as riptide.

The irony is that I have spent my life attacking and overcoming fear; as a cop the criticism most often levied at me was that I was not cautious enough. I think that's fair; I took it as a badge of honor that I didn't let being afraid stop me from doing something. In fact, it provided an extra impetus.

I've also discovered that when you refuse to give in to fear over so many years, then you stop having to make the gesture of refusing, because you stop being fearful. The trick is to remain careful and cautious without that fear as a motivation.

But I've never gone into the ocean, and I'm never going to. That has remained a riptide too far.

"You going in?" Dani asks.

"Not in this lifetime." She knows my feeling about this, but was just checking to see if I'd bite the bullet.

"What about Simon?"

"He and I have discussed it, and he shares my views on the matter."

She holds up a tennis ball, one of a half dozen that we've brought along. "Should I try?"

I nod. "Fine with me. But you're wasting your time. Simon and I are land animals."

Dani rears back and throws the ball into the water, getting it maybe thirty yards in. As she does, she yells, "Go get it, Simon."

And he does.

He plunges in like he's been doing it all his life; all he's missing is a surfboard. I have no idea how he does it, but within thirty seconds he's got the tennis ball in his mouth and is heading back to us. He drops the ball at Dani's feet, triumphant.

He looks so damn happy, and I'm glad of that. But my dominant feelings are relief that he has conquered the dreaded riptide, and guilt for having deprived him of this joy his whole life. Simon has suffered because of my reaction to something my mother said to me when I was four.

The sins of the father shall be visited upon the son.

"You learn something every day," Dani says, handing me the ball.

I throw it in, not as far as Dani did because I'm being protective of Simon. Maybe the riptide was backing off the first time, trying to make him overconfident.

He dives back in, repeating the retrieval, and this time dropping the ball at my feet. He looks at me with a combination of eagerness for me to continue the game, and disdain at my personal wimpiness.

At least that's my impression.

"Come on, let's take a walk along the water," Dani says.

"Okay."

"You going to take off your sneakers?"

It hadn't entered my mind, and I notice for the first time that Dani is barefoot. Simon is bare pawed, per usual.

"Do I have to?" I may not be the most free-spirited soul you could run into.

"Of course not; there are no sneaker police on the beach. But most people do. It feels good."

"We're walking in dirt. That feels good? I believe shoes and sneakers were originally invented to prevent people from having to walk in dirt."

"It's sand, Corey."

"That is a distinction without a difference." I think about it for a few moments, then, "Okay, what the hell."

So we have a nice barefoot walk, throwing the ball into the water along the way. I can't remember the last time I saw Simon so happy and exhausted.

"I wish I didn't have to leave," Dani says.

Dani works as an event planner, and she's doing a big corporate gathering in Miami. She'll be gone for a week. "So do I," I say. "But we'll have this dirt walk as a memory to hold on to."

When we're finished, we stop for brunch at an outdoor café. We both like to read the newspaper in situations like this; it's one of the many things I like about Dani. She's comfortable talking or not talking; it doesn't seem to matter to her either way.

We buy a *Newark Star-Ledger*; I take the sports section and she has the rest. We'll trade off as we go along. We order food; she and I each have pancakes and we get Simon a bagel and some scrambled eggs, along with a dish of water.

After a few minutes, she says, "Oh." It is not a happy *oh.*

"What's the matter?"

"A woman was murdered in Teaneck last night."

I'm a cop, or at least I was a cop. Now I'm an investigator, and I'm still interested in these things. "Let me see."

She hands me the paper and I look at the story. The entire newspaper seems to explode in my face; I read for a few moments and then lean back in my chair, trying to catch my breath.

"What's the matter?" Dani asks. "Did you know her?"

"I might have killed her."

I almost never second-guess myself. I make choices and then live with the consequences, positive or negative.

I always felt that it was part of the job of being a cop. We had to make decisions all the time, sometimes in a split second. So my view is that you do the best you can, in the time you have, and then you move on. That's been true both in my work and in my personal life.

I don't think I have looked back with regret on more than a handful of decisions I made in the twenty-five years I was a cop. But there is one that I could never wipe from my mind; one that I feared would come back to haunt me. And it has.

Lisa Yates.

The late Lisa Yates.

Lisa Yates is the reason I've called this meeting of the K Team. We call ourselves that because we're a team, and because among our members is Simon, the former K-9 cop. Okay, we're not great at team naming, but I rate us as damn good investigators.

We're meeting at Laurie's house, which is what we usually do. That way I can bring Simon, and he can play with Laurie and her husband Andy's dogs. Tara is their golden retriever, and Simon's best friend. Sebastian is their basset hound, who shows little interest in playing, or, for that matter, moving. Sebastian is into energy conservation.

Besides myself, the human members of the team are Laurie Collins and Marcus Clark. Laurie is also a former cop, a lieutenant in the Paterson police force. At one point she also went back to her hometown of Findlay, Wisconsin, where she spent a year as their police chief.

She came back because she missed the man that would eventually become her husband, Andy Carpenter. Andy is a defense attorney, and Laurie served as his chief investigator, until the K Team took over that role. Andy is a brilliant attorney, and I say that grudgingly, because he is also a major pain in the ass. Laurie's weakness for him, as far as I can tell, is her only flaw.

Marcus Clark is fairly tough to describe. You know that line about someone being the type you wouldn't want to meet in a dark alley? You wouldn't want to meet Marcus in a dark alley, or a well-lit alley, or a back alley, or a bowling alley, or an alley-oop.

Marcus is an incredibly scary guy, and he's tougher than he is scary. But he's on our side, which is quite comforting.

I haven't told Laurie and Marcus why we're meeting, but I'm going to do so now. "I don't know if you guys read about it, but a woman named Lisa Yates was murdered last Saturday night in Teaneck. She had just had dinner with a friend at Manero's. She was fired on from someone in a moving car, and two other people were also wounded. Their injuries seem not to be life threatening.

"Lisa and her dinner companion had just said good-bye, and

Lisa walked to her car. As she reached the door, she was shot twice and died at the scene."

"I read about it," Laurie says. Marcus doesn't say anything, which is no surprise because Marcus almost never says anything. When he does talk, it comes out as grunts that are indecipherable to everyone but Laurie.

"About three months before I left the force, which makes it about a year ago, there was a labor-management dispute within the department over lack of raises."

Laurie nods; she was long gone from the force at that point, but as an ex-cop I'm sure she remembers it and was supportive. It was a pretty big media story in Paterson, mainly because there was what they called a blue-out, which means that a bunch of cops called in sick in protest.

"Those of us that showed up were given assignments that weren't typical for us, depending on where the shortages were. I wound up working the streets without Simon; he got some time off. I also worked alone; there just weren't enough cops to have two in a car.

"One night I got a call for a suspected domestic violence on Derrom Avenue, on the other side of the park. A neighbor heard yelling and what sounded like a woman screaming in pain. He called nine-one-one and reported that it was not the first time this had happened.

"It was a really nice house; whoever lived there was obviously well-off. There were two people in the home, a man and woman. His name was Gerald Kline. Her name, as I'm sure you've guessed by now, was Lisa Yates. The house was owned by her.

"They claimed not to be married, but lived there together. Lisa was clearly upset and had a red welt on the side of her face.

"Both of them swore that no domestic violence had occurred, that Lisa had tripped and fell and that's how she got the bruise. I didn't believe it, not even close, so I put them in separate rooms so I could talk to her without the guy present.

"She wouldn't change her story that nothing happened and that of course therefore she would not press charges. I told her that I didn't believe her, and that I would protect her if she told me what really happened, but I got nowhere.

"I went back into the other room and told Gerald Kline that if he ever laid a finger on her again, I would beat the shit out of him, and then beat the shit out of him again, just to show that the first time wasn't a fluke. He just smiled this annoying smile; he was silently telling me that he wasn't afraid of me and would do whatever the hell he wanted. In just that brief encounter, I disliked him intensely.

"But I left because I couldn't think of anything else to do. I filed a report and that was the end of it. I still don't know what else I could have done that night, but it has bugged me ever since. Police procedure was clear, and I followed it. But I should have checked on her later on, since then, to make sure she was okay.

"So I filed a report and went on my way. And now she's dead."

"This is not something you should be blaming yourself for, Corey," Laurie says. "You did it by the book. What should you have done? Followed her for a year? Served as her bodyguard?"

"I don't know. Maybe I could have checked up on her once in a while. Maybe I could have demonstrated to her asshole boyfriend that he really had something to be afraid of. Maybe I could have done something so that she wouldn't be dead."

Marcus just shakes his head, his way of registering his disagreement with what I'm saying.

"So why are we meeting about this?" Laurie asks.

"Because I'm going to be out of commission for a while. I know we're in the middle of wrapping up two cases, but you don't need me to finish them. I need to be working on this case."

"Where are the police on it?"

"I don't know; I'm going to find out. I waited almost a week to see if they'd make a quick arrest, but since they haven't, I'm going to nail Kline myself."

"You sure it was him?"

"No way I can be sure, but he is a scumbag, and he smacked her around. So I'm guessing it's him. If I'm wrong, I'm wrong. But it will give me a lot of pleasure to hassle him regardless, and I want to catch her killer. I owe her that much."

"So where do we start?" Laurie asks.

"We don't start; I start. There's no client here. This is a freebie."

She smiles. "That's okay; money is overrated. Right, Marcus?"

"Yuhhh," Marcus says, pretty much summing up in one grunt why I like our team.

"Okay, thanks, guys. If you're sure. For now please just ask Sam Willis to find out what he can about our two main players." Sam Willis is an accountant who does investigative work for Andy Carpenter. Sam is a genius on a computer; there is virtually nothing he can't find out.

Andy, when he uses Sam, is unconcerned with whether Sam wanders into websites that are illegal to enter. When we use him, we try to avoid that, though I think he occasionally steps over the line. "Tell him nothing illegal," I add.

"Will do," Laurie says, "but Marcus and I are here and ready to do what we can."

"I know and I appreciate that," I say. "Let me nose around first."

BETWEEN us, I think Laurie and I know every cop in New Jersey.

That can come in handy in a number of ways. For example, we're unlikely to get a speeding ticket. But more important, especially in our line of work, we have access to information. In our business, information is the coin of the realm.

Today we are taking advantage of one of Laurie's contacts. We're waiting in the Suburban Diner on Route 17 in Paramus for Lieutenant Stan Battersby of Teaneck PD. Battersby works homicide, so we're looking for information on the Lisa Yates murder. He and Laurie worked together on a case back in the day, which she tells me resulted in a conviction.

It's lunchtime so the place is crowded. We have a table near the back, but we can see the entrance. A guy comes in and I immediately know it's Battersby; cops just carry themselves differently. Battersby might as well have I'M A COP tattooed on his forehead.

Laurie sees him as well and waves him over. They hug hello and she introduces us. He sits down and Laurie asks if he's hungry.

"Who's buying?" he asks.

"We are," I say.

He smiles and smacks his hands together in anticipation. "Let's get some menus over here."

We all order, and then I have to sit through ten minutes of them reminiscing about the case they worked on. Cases that end with an arrest and conviction generally lead to greater reflection. Nostalgia works that way.

"You still living with that asshole?" Battersby asks.

"If you're by chance referring to Andy, we're married with an eleven-year-old son."

He laughs. "You married him even though you knew I was available?"

Laurie returns the laugh. "I don't know what I was thinking."

Andy Carpenter is probably New Jersey's most famous defense attorney. In achieving that prominence, he has pretty much alienated every police officer on the East Coast. That Laurie is his wife doesn't even matter, and she has to deal with comments like this fairly consistently.

I include myself in that alienation; our history consisted of an unpleasant cross-examination in an otherwise-now-forgotten trial. It did not go well for me, but I only hold grudges until I die, and maybe a couple of years after that.

"We want to talk to you about the Lisa Yates murder," I say.

He nods. "Tough one."

"How so?"

"It was likely a professional hit, but there is nothing about her that would seem to warrant that. And the other two that were wounded seem like innocent bystanders as well. Yates was a nine to fiver; she doesn't fit the profile, but I think she was the target."

"Why do you say that?"

"Two bullets: one in the head and one in the heart. Perfect placement. The other two people each got it in the leg. My hunch is that they were hit to make it look like a random shooting. Though my captain disagrees."

"What does he think?"

"That it was just a drive-by. Random violence, anyone could have been the target. My captain is full of shit."

"What about Gerald Kline?" I ask.

"What about him?"

The waitress comes over to serve the food, so I wait for her to leave before answering. By this time Battersby is deep into his open hot roast beef sandwich, and gravy is dripping from his mouth.

"Gerald Kline is her boyfriend, or at least he was. I was called to her house in Paterson on a DV about a year and a half ago; he had smacked her and drawn blood."

This gets Battersby to put down his fork. "I know who Kline is. But your DV report wasn't in the record."

"I filed it; I'm surprised it didn't work its way to you. But it never went anywhere. She wouldn't press charges and they both denied the whole thing. She said she fell."

He frowns. "Women seem to fall and walk into doors a lot, especially the ones that hang out with asshole men. I've checked out Kline, but he has an alibi for that night. He was giving a seminar on something or other on Long Island."

"That doesn't mean he didn't hire someone," I say.

"No, it doesn't. But that doesn't really fit the domestic violence pattern."

"Do you mind if we get involved?" Laurie asks.

Battersby immediately looks wary. "Define involved."

"We investigate the case, but we do it without stepping on

your toes. Any actionable information we get, we turn over to you."

"You have a client somewhere in this?"

"No," I say, "just a desire to see justice done."

The light goes on in his eyes. "You're blaming yourself for not making an arrest on the DV? Come on, you know that's bullshit."

"Kline is a piece of garbage. He was laughing at me that night, as much as telling me that he could do whatever he wanted, and I couldn't touch him. So right now I want to touch him; in fact, I want to strangle him. There's no law against that, is there?"

Battersby laughs. "Go for it."

"So to get back to the original question," Laurie says. "Do you mind if we get involved?"

"What if I mind?" Battersby asks.

"We'll get involved anyway. But we'll be less forthcoming with information."

He shrugs his acceptance. "All hands on deck. But give me a couple of days to talk to Kline again before you beat the shit out of him."

"Deal," I say. "You want dessert?"

Battersby nods. "Damn straight. And I think we should have regular lunch meetings to discuss the case."

DANI is in control of our relationship.

I'm not superhappy about that, and I'm sure not used to it, but just that I'm sitting here at home, thinking about her while she is away on business, is highly unusual for me.

I don't think this has ever happened to me before. For the most part, I've never been in a relationship long enough to lose control. In the past I always quickly felt claustrophobic, so I would find a reason to bail out. I'm really good at finding bail-out rationales.

But with Dani it's been different. I was all set to end it. . . . I fully expected to do so . . . but I could never find the reason. I just couldn't pull the trigger. That's because she's presented one big, so far insurmountable, challenge.

I like her.

A lot. I never thought I could like someone this much.

If a young guy came to me looking for relationship advice,

though he would have to be flat-out nuts to do so, I would tell him to find someone he wasn't too crazy about. That's the key. That way, if you dump her, or if she dumps you, what's the big deal?

Somehow Dani is different, and I haven't quite figured out exactly how. And I'm not talking about the obvious facts that she's funny and smart and beautiful. It's something else that's caused me to lower my defenses.

Soon I'm going to analyze it, even though it's way too late. The enemy has scaled the wall, taken over, and planted her flag. I am a relationship POW.

"Simon, how could you let this happen to me?"

I talk to Simon a lot. We're buddies, and even though I doubt he understands most of what I say, he's a good listener. I think he's probably listening for the word *biscuit,* but I can't be sure.

Simon is smart; he was the best police dog in the department, and it wasn't even close. We had a connection between us when we were on the job; we knew what each other needed, and we never failed to provide it. He was the best cop in the department, including me.

Right now it's time to stop thinking about Dani and start thinking about Gerald Kline. Lieutenant Battersby said that Kline has an alibi for the night of Lisa Yates's death, which doesn't surprise me.

If it was a professional hit, then the killer was hired. If you're going to hire someone to commit a murder, it makes perfect sense to do it at a time when you have an ironclad alibi. That's actually the reason that alibis exist.

Battersby is right that domestic violence murders don't usually involve hired killers, but there are no ironclad rules. If you have enough money and want someone dead, but don't have the guts to do it yourself, you hire someone. Kline struck me as a gutless worm.

I've come to the conclusion that our investigation has to pro-
ceed on two tracks. One, obviously, is to try to find evidence of
Kline's guilt. That is not the best way to investigate a case. It's
generally a bad idea to decide in advance who the guilty party
is, then try to make the pieces fit. The evidence should call the
shots; the investigator should just follow it to a conclusion.

I admit that my visceral dislike for Kline is driving me. I think
he's guilty and I want him to be guilty; I just have to keep those
feelings in check and be as impartial as I can.

The other track we have to follow is Lisa Yates's life, and
not only her relationship with Kline. Was there someone else
that might have wanted her dead? Someone with money and connections? We know absolutely nothing about Lisa, but that will
change in a hurry.

"Simon, you on board for this?" Simon just looks blankly at
me, so I add, "There are going to be biscuits involved."

That perks him up, so I head for the biscuit jar to demonstrate
that this is not an empty promise. This is a ritual we played out
every morning before going to work on the force.

As I give him one, I say, "Not sure what your role will be yet,
but stay ready."

He barks his agreement, or maybe he's barking for another
biscuit. I give him another, then a third.

"Good. Glad to have you on board."

"YEAH, I remember that night. It was the only time I called the cops."

I'm talking to Walter Nichols, Lisa Yates's neighbor. He made the 911 call that resulted in my trip to the Yates house that night . . . the night I didn't do anything except write a meaningless report.

He continues, "A cop showed up; I saw him go in. But he came back out after about a half hour, and I don't know what happened."

"I was the cop."

"I thought you said you were private. You're a cop?"

"That was then; this is now. Tell me about Lisa Yates."

"I don't know that much about her. I just saw her outside a few times, mostly when I was mowing my lawn. I haven't lived here that long. She liked to garden, so if she was out there, we just exchanged small talk."

"When was the last time you saw her?"

He thinks for a moment. "It's been a while; come to think of it, I haven't see her car either. Maybe she's away?"

Based on what he just said, he obviously hasn't heard that she was murdered. It has not been a huge story in the media.

"You told the nine-one-one operator that there were other incidents in her house, and you just said that it was the 'only time you called the cops.' Tell me about the other incidents, and why you chose to call that night."

"Can I ask why you're asking me this now?"

"Fair question. Lisa Yates was murdered last week."

He reacts; obviously stunned by the news. "Holy shit." Then, "Was that her, that thing at the restaurant?"

"Yes, it was. Now please tell me about the other incidents."

He shakes his head in amazement; still processing the news he's just heard. Finally, "They were arguments more than anything else. Really loud arguments, but I didn't get the feeling it was physical. You understand, I wasn't prying. I usually heard it when I was walking my dog."

"I understand. Did you get a sense of what they were arguing about?"

"Not really. One time I heard him yell, 'You'll do it my way.' Or, 'You'll do what you're told.' Something like that; it was hard to tell exactly."

"But that night was different?"

He nods. "Yes. She screamed, like she was in pain, or like she had been hit. Was I right?"

"It works better if I ask the questions," I say. Then, "You were right."

He nods sadly. "How can guys do stuff like that?"

"That's not something I have an answer for. Do you know if she had any close friends in the neighborhood?"

He shrugs. "I have no idea. This area isn't like that, you know? I mean, basically we wave to each other. But that could be just me; maybe everybody is close but they shut me out." He shakes his head. "But I don't think so."

"LET'S start with Gerald Kline," Sam Willis says.

Sam is giving his report on what he has learned about Kline and Lisa Yates from his relatively quick computer search. Once again we're having this meeting at Laurie's house, in deference to Simon and Tara's close relationship. Since Tara and Simon have long ago been "fixed," as a doting parent I can be confident that their friendship will remain platonic.

Laurie has prevailed on Andy to go out and get us some pizzas. He wasn't thrilled about it, but he certainly prefers it to being involved in our case. Andy is wealthy; I'm told it's as a result of an inheritance, as well as some lucrative cases. Not having to work, he has become a lawyer who tries to avoid lawyering at all costs.

"Kline lives in Ridgewood," Sam says, "house is worth two million seven. He's a headhunter; he recruits people for jobs in the medical services industry. But he does more than that; I'm not sure how to describe it yet."

"What do you mean?"

"Well, he gives seminars. People pay to come hear him speak, sometimes for an entire weekend. They have lectures, workshops, that kind of stuff. As far as I can tell, it's all tied in. The people are there to learn how to make themselves good prospects for jobs. How to interview, do a résumé, learn about the industry, et cetera."

"Does he recruit from the people at his seminars?" Laurie asks.

Sam shrugs. "Not sure; no way to tell from what I'm looking at. Kline has his own firm; it's just Kline, his partner, and one assistant.

"He seems to do very well; his net worth just from what I can find is in excess of seven million dollars. There could be a lot more that's hidden, but I haven't looked that deep.

"He's forty-one . . . never been married. Father is deceased, mother lives in Toledo, where he grew up. No siblings. Got an undergraduate degree from Stony Brook, MBA from Marshall.

"One interesting item: in the last two months he's cashed three checks, two for nine thousand dollars and one for seven thousand. Not sure what he did with the cash, but that's not surprising. The main reason to use cash is to avoid records. The main reason for doing it in nine–thousand-dollar increments is that the bank is required to report ten-thousand-dollar-and-higher cash transactions to the government."

"How do you know about the cashed checks?" I ask, already knowing the answer.

"I accessed his bank records."

"Legally?"

"Oops. I tried to stay on this side of the line, but sometimes the line is blurred."

"If you see a blurry line, you probably shouldn't cross it. Anything else on Kline?"

"Not so far. You want to hear about Lisa Yates?"

"Of course."

"She was thirty-six when she died; would have been thirty-seven today."

Laurie shakes her head in sadness. I know that she's feeling, in the grand scheme of life, it is utterly meaningless that today is Lisa Yates's birthday, but it still feels extra-awful.

Sam continues, "She was born in Garfield and grew up there. She went to Rutgers and got a BA in computer science. She taught computer programming for a while and then three years ago she went to work for Ardmore Medical Systems."

"What is that?"

"It's apparently a firm that tracks and maintains medical records. You know how when you go to a specialist they already have your records? Ardmore facilitates that process. They probably do a lot more than that; I just haven't gotten into it."

"You said Kline recruited in the health-care industry. Did he place her in that job?"

"I don't know. I would have no way to access that. Moving right along, she's lived on Derrom Avenue in Paterson for the past two and a half years."

"That's where I met her," I say.

"But strangely, it looks like she's been living in a motel in East Rutherford for the past month."

"What makes you say that?" Laurie asks.

"She's paid for it for that long. I suppose she could have been paying for someone else, but it seems a likelier bet that it was for herself."

"How do you know this?" I ask.

"Her credit card records."

"Ah . . . another blurry line."

Sam puts on a fake frown. "Damn those things."

Andy comes in carrying six large pizzas. Four of them are for Marcus; he doesn't talk much but he sure can eat. "Here we go," Andy says. "Is the K Team planning on reimbursing me for the pizzas?"

"As the team treasurer," I say, "I can pretty much rule that out. But I do have a legal question."

"Uh-oh."

"If we skip our investigation and I just strangle Kline with my bare hands, can you get me off?"

Andy thinks for a moment. "I could, but would choose not to."

With that he goes to get Ricky, Laurie and Andy's eleven-year-old son, so he can share in the pizza. While I have never been a big fan of Andy's, going back to that cross-examination, Laurie and Ricky are crazy about him, which I consider pretty significant.

And as long as he keeps buying the pizza, we might even become buddies.

THERE'S a memorial service for Lisa Yates at a funeral home in Elmwood Park today.

It was listed in the paper yesterday. It drives the cop in me nuts; public announcements like that are an invitation to burglars to rob the house of the deceased and close family members, since it's a sure bet that no one will be home. It happens all the time.

For us, the service is a good way to find out who was close to Lisa; it will serve as an early guide for who we should be talking with. We're looking to see who is invited up to give remarks; passing acquaintances don't get that honor.

I'm also looking to see if Gerald Kline shows up. It certainly wouldn't prove anything either way, but it will give me a chance to renew my hatred firsthand.

I scan the room when we arrive, but I don't see Kline among the eighty-one attendees. I have this weird mental need and ability to count things in clusters or groups; I can do it quickly and accurately. I also can instantly count the number of letters in spoken sentences. I used to do it in an attempt to amuse people at parties, which may well be why people stopped inviting me to parties.

The first person to speak is clearly a member of the clergy. I don't have any idea what religious faith he represents; he's not wearing a uniform with the team name on his jersey.

He talks about Lisa in general terms, occasionally throwing in a meaningless specific. I would bet anything that he never met her, and that he did a quick cram course with a member of her family a few minutes ago. It bugs me; someone who lived for almost four decades should not have a stranger speaking about her.

When he's done, Lisa's sister, Denise, takes her place at the podium. She talks movingly about their growing up together; Lisa was Denise's "big sister" and was apparently protective of her. She says that Lisa gave her great advice about everything, including men. She smiles ruefully and says, "I should have listened." This gets a good laugh from the crowd; in my experience crowds will look for pretty much any excuse to laugh during funeral services.

Next up is Una Loge, who tearfully talks about Lisa, describing her as "my best friend." Una reveals that she was the one who had dinner with Lisa that horrible night, accurately describing the events as senseless and horrible. She talks about how her faith teaches her to forgive and forget, but when it comes to the person who did this, "I will never forgive, and I certainly will never forget."

Una seems to have much more to say, but she keeps breaking into tears, and another woman comes up and leads her off the stage.

The last speaker is Susan Redick, a coworker of Lisa's. It is clear that she was not as close to Lisa as were the previous two speakers. She talks of Lisa as a good friend; someone who kept things lively and happy in the office. You could always count on Lisa, according to Susan, no matter how hectic or tense things got.

Once she is finished, an announcement is made as to where the funeral will be, and that everyone is invited. We have no intention or need to go there; we've learned all we're going to learn.

Laurie and I head to the exits; we're going to try to follow Susan Redick and Una Loge to their cars. We'll get their license plate numbers, which will in turn give us their addresses and phone numbers. It's likely that Lisa's sister, Denise, will be in one of the funeral home cars, but we'll still get her address later.

I also watch for Gerald Kline again, just in case I didn't see him in the chapel. There's still no sign of him. He's not here, probably too deep in mourning for the woman he smacked around.

I hate that I can no longer bring Simon everywhere.

When we were cops, we were joined at the hip. He was my partner, and rarely did I not have him with me on the job. That night at Lisa Yates's house was an unfortunate, notable exception. If Simon had been there that night, he would have disliked Kline as much as I did. In a perfect world he would have taken a juicy bite out of his leg.

As a large German shepherd, Simon could be intimidating, especially since he did not do much smiling when he was working. That intimidation usually worked in our favor, but it would be counterproductive at a time like this. I'm going to talk to Denise Yates, Lisa's younger sister. Laurie has set up the meeting; she has a way of getting people to be willing to talk.

I take Simon for an extra long walk before leaving, as a way of making it up to him. It doesn't work; he is clearly pissed at me when I head out without him.

It is going to come as a surprise to Denise to see me show up; she's expecting Laurie. If I had Simon with me, it might kill the interview. Laurie had said that Denise was hesitant to agree to meet in the first place and offered to come along. I said it wasn't necessary; that I would use my dazzling charm to win Denise over.

To my surprise, she wanted to meet at Lisa's home on Derrom Avenue. I've been here before, and that previous visit is the reason that I'm working this case at all. Standing at the bottom of the steps and looking up at the entrance does not bring back pleasant memories.

I ring the bell and Denise comes to the door. Her eyes are red; my guess is that she has done quite a bit of crying since her sister was murdered.

"Oh," she says, when I identify myself. "I was expecting Laurie Collins."

"Laurie is my partner. We're both working this case. I hope that's okay."

She thinks about it, like it just might not be okay, but finally says I can come in. We enter, and I'm struck by how little has changed, and how indelibly the place is carved into my memory.

"This is Lisa's house," she says, not realizing that I already know that. "I have to go through some of her papers. I know if I put it off, I'll never do it. I'm not up to going through the rest of her things; that's for another day." She pauses. "I'm actually glad not to be alone."

"I appreciate your talking to me. I'll try not to take too much of your time."

"What is your interest in this?"

"We're trying to find Lisa's killer."

"Why? Are you working with the police?"

"Not officially, but we've talked to them."

"Is somebody paying you?"

I need to be up-front with this woman, so I tell her the truth about the reason for my interest in the case. I end with "I feel I may have let her down that night, and I want to know if that led to what happened."

She nods. "I understand. If there's any way I can help . . ."

"Do you know Gerald Kline?"

She frowns. "Yes."

"Tell me about his relationship with Lisa."

"He controlled her; it used to drive me crazy. Lisa was a strong, independent woman, except around that man. He had a way about him."

"What do you mean?"

"He could be charming. I mean, he ran these seminars and it was literally his job to be charming. But it could be powerful, and Lisa couldn't handle it."

"Was she afraid of him?"

"I wouldn't say that, but it's possible. We were really close and we talked about everything . . . everything except Gerald Kline. Lisa knew how I felt about him, so we just avoided it. It made things awkward, as you can imagine. But we got through it."

"Did Lisa ever express any fear of anyone? Any physical fear?"

"Why? Do you think they were after Lisa? According to the newspaper accounts, the police seem to think it was just some random animals shooting from a car."

"That's possible. But it works best for us to assume she was the target. If it turns out that she wasn't, then we'll adjust. So did she ever seem afraid of anyone? Like she might be in danger?"

"No, but she had been acting strangely lately. We talked some, but she was cut off more than usual. I thought it might be problems at work, so I didn't push it."

"So you're not aware of any enemies she might have had?"

"Lisa? Lisa was the friendliest, most wonderful person you could ever meet. She did not have an enemy in the world."

The one thing that all murder victims have in common, as described by their friends and family, is that they never had an enemy in the world. I rarely point out that someone killed them, an act that some would think might qualify them as an enemy.

I ask Denise to please call me if she thinks of anything that might be relevant to the case. She promises to do so.

I leave, having accomplished as little during this trip to the house as I did during my last one.

LAURIE and I are going to talk with Una Loge together.

I told Laurie that both of us doing it was overkill, but her response was that she should do it and I should stay home. "She's really fragile and shaken up," Laurie says. "It wasn't easy to get her willing to talk."

The unspoken implication was that Laurie can handle matters with more sensitivity than me. She's saying that because she can handle matters with more sensitivity than me. On the sensitivity level, I probably rank just below Mike Tyson.

She didn't want us to come to her home, so we're meeting at a Starbucks. Una is waiting for us when we arrive; I recognize her from the funeral service. She's sitting at an outdoor table, but two other occupied tables are nearby. "Why don't we sit over there?" I point to a table near the side. "We can talk more privately there."

So we move over. I head in to get coffees for all of us, leaving

Laurie to make Una comfortable. By the time I get back, they are smiling like good buddies. Laurie has that way about her.

"I got some scones also in case anyone wants one." I put down the coffee and scones.

"No thanks," Laurie says, and Una turns them down as well.

"Perfect. I was hoping to have all of them for myself."

Laurie says, "Una, I know this is difficult, but we want to ask you questions about Lisa, and about that night."

"It was horrible."

"Tell us what happened, please."

Una takes a deep breath. "There really isn't that much to tell. We had dinner and said good-bye at the door. I had parked with the valet, and she parked on the street. I was waiting for my car when I heard these loud noises; I didn't know what they were, maybe firecrackers.

"Then people were screaming and running in all directions. I ran back into the restaurant with some other people; I wasn't even sure why. Then somebody said they were gunshots.

"All of a sudden the police were there and they questioned all of us about what we saw. All this time I didn't even think about Lisa; I had no idea that she was . . . that she was . . . one of the victims. I called her when I got home to tell her what happened.

"She didn't answer, so I started to get worried. Then I turned on the news and I found out. . . . I still can't believe it. It seems surreal."

"Did she act normally during your dinner?" I ask. "Did she seem concerned about anything, or even afraid?"

Una seems surprised by the question. "Why? You don't think she was the target, that they were after her, do you?"

"We're investigating all possibilities," Laurie asks.

"Okay, but I can't imagine anyone wanting to hurt Lisa."

"How did she act during the dinner?"

Una thinks about it for a few moments. "Well, I guess she seemed a little distant. When I asked her about it, she mentioned some problems at work. I used to work there and she usually shared stuff about the office with me, but this time she didn't want to."

"Do you know Gerald Kline?" Laurie asks. I would have asked the same question, but my mouth is full with the second scone.

Una frowns. "I do."

"You don't like him?"

"I didn't like the way he treated her. He controlled her; he thinks he controls everything."

It's the same way that Lisa's sister described Kline and his relationship with Lisa. "Why didn't she break it off with him?" I ask.

Una looks surprised again. "What do you mean? She did, like six weeks ago. I don't know what took her so long."

"They split up?" Laurie asks, and Una nods in response.

"Did she say anything about it? Maybe describe why, or what happened?" I ask.

"Not really. Just that it was over, and that she was glad about it. She said it was time to move on, to make major changes in her life." Then, "She never got that chance."

"She didn't express a fear of him? That he might hurt her?"

Una looks around, as if someone might be listening in. "I shouldn't be saying this; she asked me never to talk about it. But I guess circumstances have changed."

"What is it?" Laurie asks.

"He hit her, once. She told me about it when it happened. She said the police came to the house, but she denied it. She made up a story. I told her she had to get rid of that guy, that if it happened once, it would happen again. But it never did, or if it did, she never told me about it. And she would tell me everything."

"The police didn't do anything?" I ask, unfortunately knowing the answer, and I'm not sure why I need to hear it reinforced. Laurie frowns at the question; she probably doesn't know why I continue to beat myself up. I'm not sure myself.

Una shakes her head. "No. Lisa said the officer just asked some questions and left."

ALL that Gerald Kline did with this particular cell phone was answer it when it rang.

They had given it to him only to answer their calls. He was not to make outgoing calls, except to one person, and was not to text or do anything else with it. He had his own phone for all of that.

Only one person ever called him. He referred to himself as Carlos, but Kline did not know if that was his real name. The people Carlos represented, and perhaps Carlos himself, were brilliant. Kline had never been associated with anyone like them; they knew everything and could do everything. And they paid him well . . . very, very well.

The call came when Kline was at home. The phone had a distinctive ring, and since it rang so infrequently, it never failed to jar him. These calls were always important, never casual, and they made Kline nervous.

Carlos never bothered with "hello"; he considered it a waste of time. "Someone is watching you, checking you out."

The statement caught Kline by surprise. "Who?"

"At this point we don't know. They are very good at what they do and so far are successfully concealing their identity."

If Carlos said they were good, Kline knew, then they were damn good. "What are they looking for?"

"Everything. Your history. Your finances. Everything. Who would be doing this?"

"I have no idea."

"That is not an acceptable response. You must have triggered something with your activities."

"I haven't done anything out of the ordinary. I swear."

"Think about it; there is something. I want to hear from you soon."

Click.

Kline got off the phone worried. Not about the people who were checking on him, but about Carlos and his people. Kline did not want to do anything to annoy them; this was not a job he could afford to lose.

The money was too damn good.

"I hate to say this, but we just may be spinning our wheels," Laurie says.

I know what she means. Lisa seems to have been fairly tight-lipped about her relationship with Kline, which means we are unlikely to get any incriminating information about him from Lisa's family and friends. While they did not like him, they didn't discuss it much with Lisa.

That means our only hope is to tie Kline to the actual shooter.

"You have any suggestions?"

Laurie nods. "Just one. We go straight at Kline; we tell him that we're onto him and that we're going to nail him. Then we watch him, monitor his calls, and see how he reacts. Maybe we'll get nothing from it, but we might scare him. That in itself would be some satisfaction, wouldn't it?"

"It would. I think it's a good idea."

"Good. I'll get Marcus on it. He can figure out the best way to go at him. And I'll get Sam on the phone stuff."

I know what she means about "phone stuff." Sam will break into the phone company computers and monitor who Kline calls, especially in the period right after we confront him.

It's illegal, which troubles me greatly. Andy is always fine with it; Laurie somewhat less so. Their argument is that if it ever got into court, we could subpoena the same records legally; this just gives us a needed head start. I've reluctantly gone along with it in the past, and I'm sure I will cave again in this instance.

I nod. "Okay, thanks. I'm looking forward to meeting Mr. Kline again."

"I'll go with you."

"No. I can handle it."

"You shouldn't be alone; there's no telling what might happen."

"I won't be alone; I'll have Simon with me. If you're there when I beat the shit out of him, it will make me self-conscious. It's a guy thing."

"I know you're kidding. You are kidding, right?"

"I am. Mostly."

Laurie calls Sam first, and before she can give him the new assignment, he says he wants to come over and give a report on where he is now. In the meantime, I go home to get Simon.

I've been feeling guilty leaving him alone so much; he's not used to it. He's a working dog who loved his job, and I don't think this partial retirement is coming easy for him.

I've thought about getting him a friend, and I've notified the K-9 department that if any dogs reach retirement age, and their handlers don't want them, then I would take them. I doubt it will happen; most handlers feel about their dogs like I feel about Simon. Giving him up was and is completely inconceivable.

I get Simon and go back to Laurie's. When we pull up to the house, Simon perks up immediately. He knows this is where Tara lives. Simon needs a friend.

Sam is already here and talking with Laurie. "What did I miss?" I ask.

"Sam was just telling me that the Mets stink. It was fascinating."

"Is that the highlight of your report, Sam?"

He nods. "Pretty much. I've looked in to Stanley and Katherine Branstetter, the other two people shot the night Lisa Yates was killed. By the way, they're both out of the hospital.

"They live in New City, up in Rockland County, and they own and operate Kate's Diner in Spring Valley. No criminal record, no obvious associations with people we would be interested in, and they have a net worth of seven hundred thousand, most of which is their house.

"They have two kids, both have graduated college and are currently living out of state. There is nothing I can find about the Branstetter family that would make them a likely target of a hit man."

"On the surface, the same thing would be true for Lisa Yates," Laurie says, and Sam nods his agreement.

"So we're back where we were," I say. "I confront Kline, we rattle his cage, and we see what happens. Sam, I'm going to meet with Kline. We'll want to know who he calls, if anyone, in the twenty-four hours after that meeting. Can you do that?"

"Of course. Laurie already told me about it."

"How will you get his phone numbers?"

"Duh," Sam says, as Laurie smiles.

"Okay. I don't want to know anyway. As soon as Marcus figures out the best time and place, we do it."

I hate waiting, which is among the reasons why I like Marcus.

There is nothing casual about Marcus when he gets an assignment; he does it and moves on to the next thing.

He has quickly come up with a time and place for me to confront Kline. Like Laurie, he also offers to come with me. There is no doubt that five minutes in a room with Marcus would make Kline confess to killing Lisa Yates. He would also confess to the Kennedy assassination, the Lindbergh kidnapping, and the sinking of the *Lusitania*.

I probably would also.

But I decline Marcus's participation, just as I declined Laurie's. I'm sure they are waiting for me to call if there's an emergency, and they're probably stationed nearby. That's what I would do if the roles were reversed; it's what teammates do.

But I sized Kline up that night at Lisa Yates's house; he does not represent a threat to me. If I can't handle him, I shouldn't just be retired. I should be in a retirement home.

Marcus suggested I wait at Kline's house for him. For the last two nights he has left his office in Fort Lee, gone to a bar/restaurant near his office for dinner and a couple of drinks, and then driven to his Ridgewood home.

He has been considerate enough to live in an upscale neighborhood, with good distance separating him from his nearest neighbors. It's also dark; apparently rich people don't like streetlights.

I park down the block from Kline's house, and Simon and I walk toward it and then up his fairly long driveway. We won't be seen from the street, and Kline will have no idea we are here. He'll find out soon enough.

Kline arrives ten minutes earlier than Marcus predicted. He parks in the detached garage, and Simon and I are waiting for him when he exits and heads for the house. A floodlight is on, obviously triggered by a motion detector.

"Hello, Gerald."

He just about jumps out of his skin, letting out some guttural noise, and his knees actually seem to buckle. When he gets control, he says, "Who are you? What's going on? I have nothing worth robbing."

As he finishes saying this, he sees Simon, who has his game face on. Simon is obviously not here to play fetch. "Holy shit," Kline says. "Come on, tell me what's happening."

"You don't recognize me?"

"No. Should I?"

"My name is Corey Douglas. I was there the night you smacked Lisa Yates around."

He struggles to make the connection. "Douglas . . . the cop."

"Right. The cop."

"Why are you here?"

"Because I'm going to nail you for killing her."

"Hey, come on. I had nothing to do with that."

"Right. Like you didn't hit her that night."

"Okay, maybe I pushed her and she fell. She was driving me crazy. She knew it was as much her fault as mine, which is why she didn't press charges. But I didn't kill her . . . come on, man. I talked to the police; I wasn't even in town that night."

"I know about the twenty-five grand in cash, and I know who you paid it to. You're going down, and I'm going to enjoy watching it."

"I'm telling you, you're wrong. That cash was to go play blackjack in Atlantic City. Lisa and I broke up a while ago; why would I kill her?"

I can feel myself getting angry; it's an anger I have been carrying a long time. I move toward him slightly . . . threatening. It's a subtle threat but not an empty one; I'm not sure what I might do.

"I'm just spitballing here, but it could be because you're a chickenshit asshole. Why did you break up? She got tired of being abused?"

"Because she dumped my ass." Then he shrugged. "She caught me fooling around. It was time to move on anyway. We both knew it."

"Don't get too comfortable, Kline. I'm coming for you, and I'm not moving on. And I'm no longer a cop; I'm private. So I can do whatever I want with you."

With that I turn and leave. I have to tug on Simon's leash; he's staring at Kline like he wants to use him for a chew toy.

That's my boy.

LAURIE and Marcus are waiting for Simon and me at Laurie's house after we leave Kline's.

I'm going to update them on what happened, which shouldn't take long, since nothing of great consequence was discovered. And I'm sure Simon is planning to check in with Tara.

"He denied it," I say. "Which was obviously to be expected. The surprising thing is he admitted to the domestic violence, sort of. He said he pushed her, and she fell."

"Maybe he just wanted to give you something," Laurie says. "Maybe he was afraid of the lunatic and his dog waiting for him behind his house."

"That's the strange thing. He was scared when he first saw me, but when he realized who I was and why I was there, it was almost like he was relieved."

"Could be that knowing you were a cop gave him confidence you wouldn't do anything violent to him?"

I think about that for a few seconds. "It's possible, but that's not what it felt like. It was almost as if he was afraid I might be someone else, someone who he was really afraid of. Although his level of nervousness went up a bit when I told him I knew about the cash he withdrew."

"So where are we now?" Laurie asks.

"The same nowhere we were before." It's hard for me to admit that, but it's true. "Unless he makes a phone call that helps us and Sam tracks it."

"If not, then much as I hate to say it, it might be time for a reality check, Corey."

I nod. "Let her rip. I can take it."

"Okay . . . here goes. We have not been able to lay a glove on him. I'm not saying we've exhausted all our possibilities; there are still plenty of people to talk to. But all we've uncovered so far are the suspicious cash withdrawals, which could be explained in a hundred different ways."

I nod. "He said he was using it to gamble in Atlantic City."

"There's plenty more to do, and Marcus and I are happy to follow your lead. But I don't think there is any concrete reason to think he did it, other than your dislike for him. We're not aware of any other domestic violence incidents between them, and if that were a recurring problem, there would be records of it somewhere.

"They dated for a while and they split up; why would we think that would lead to murder? And a professional hit from a moving car? Do we have any evidence that Kline had connections to that world?

"We don't even know for sure that Lisa Yates was the target. It could have been the other couple, or it could have been someone else there that escaped injury, or it could have been a case of mistaken identity.

"We just don't know, and we're not likely to know."

The phone rings and Laurie gets it. After hello, she says, "Thanks, Sam. Stay on it, please."

She hangs up. "Sam says that Kline hasn't made any calls since you left."

"Okay," I say. "Let me think about this for a little while."

"Take your time," Laurie says. "We are ready and willing to take this as far as you want to. Your instincts have always been excellent."

I smile. "Not just mine. Simon couldn't stand him either."

Laurie laughs. "You sound like Andy. If Tara doesn't like someone, Andy thinks the person is a serial killer. Of course, Tara likes everyone." Then, more serious, "We'll await your direction, right, Marcus?"

Marcus nods. "Yunhh."

That pretty much sums it up.

"I found out what is going on. We have nothing to worry about," Kline said.

He had felt this news was important enough to make one of his rare calls on the special phone that they had given him.

As always happened when he called Carlos, the call went unanswered, and there was no option to leave a message. Yet within a minute Carlos returned the call. Kline had no idea why Carlos went through this process but assumed there must be a good reason. Carlos always seemed to have a good reason for everything.

"That will require some explanation," Carlos said.

"Sure. A while back, when I was living with Lisa . . . with Yates . . . we had an argument. I got pissed and I hit her. Only time I ever did it, and I didn't hit her that hard. Anyway, a neighbor must have heard what was going on, because next thing we know a cop shows up." Kline was relaxing into the story, knowing it will relieve the pressure.

"Lisa knew better than to go against me, against us, so she told the cop she fell. He left, but I could tell he didn't believe us. He was obviously pissed that there was nothing he could do, and I let him know he couldn't touch me.

"Anyway, this same cop showed up with a scary dog at my house tonight. He thinks I killed Yates because of what happened that night. Of course I told him I didn't."

"What was his response to that?"

"I think he believed me, but . . ." Kline caught himself, but realized he had made a major error.

"But what?"

"Well, I had taken some cash out of the bank, twenty-five grand, and somehow he knew about it. He must be the guy checking up on me, like you said."

"Why did you take out that cash?"

Kline knew the question was coming, but he didn't have a good answer for it. He was aware he was about to dig a deeper hole, but he had no alternative. "To pay some of my people. But I lied and told him it was to play blackjack in Atlantic City. He believed me."

"We supply the funds. At this point you still do not know that?"

"No, I do. . . . I know that. But the money was late, and my people were getting anxious. I didn't want to bother you, so I paid them and reimbursed myself when your money arrived."

"Tell me everything you know about this policeman."

"Well, for one thing, he's not a cop anymore. I guess he retired or something. And he had a dog that looked like a police dog . . . scary as hell."

"His name?"

"Corey Douglas."

"I will be calling you very soon."

"Okay." Kline grew concerned; this conversation had not gone in a direction he had anticipated. "Is there anything wrong? I really think it's under control."

"Former cop Corey Douglas may have to be dealt with."

I'M mostly resigned to the fact that I'm not getting anywhere.

Laurie is right; not only do we have little chance to nail Kline for the murder, but there is an excellent possibility that he had nothing to do with it. I know that I have been letting my dislike for him color my attitude.

I don't feel bad about it; if I was still a cop, then having this kind of bias would be unacceptable. But in my current role, I can take a flier on something like this without causing any harm. But I should not be dragging Laurie and Marcus deeper into it.

I've got an already scheduled interview today, which I am going to keep, with Susan Redick. Redick was the fourth speaker at Lisa Yates's funeral service; she worked with her at Ardmore Medical Systems.

I take Simon on our morning walk, and when I get back, the phone is ringing. It's Dani calling from Miami; we've only talked twice this past week, and I've missed it.

She's calling to tell me that she'll be back on Sunday and that she's looking forward to it, because, according to her, "it's a hundred and thirty-eight degrees in the shade here, although there isn't any shade. And I went for one of those beach dirt walks you like so much and burned my feet."

Dani says that she's going to come to my house from the airport, which I'm happy to hear. She's been living at my place a little more than half the time, while still keeping her own apartment. It's working out well, so neither of us is inclined to make any changes.

When I get off the phone, Simon and I head out. It's Saturday, so Susan Redick asked me to come to her house in Leonia. I had checked with her to see if she liked dogs, and she said she loved them. She has two of her own, and apparently they would be excited to meet a new friend.

Susan and her two dogs are waiting for us on her front porch when we arrive. She has one dog in each arm, and it doesn't look like she's straining to carry them. That's because one is a Maltese, whom she introduces as Tamar, and the other one is a Pomeranian named Ginny. Simon could have them both for lunch and still be hungry afterward.

"Look, a new friend," she says.

"You sure they're going to be okay with Simon?"

"You said he was dog friendly, right?"

"Right. But he's used to actual full-size dogs. I'm afraid he could step on one of them by accident."

She laughs. "They can handle themselves. Come on in."

Once we get inside, she puts the minidogs on the floor. Simon has no idea what to make of them as they run circles around him. It is hilarious. Then they all run into another room, or, more accurately, they chase Simon into the other room.

"Don't look so worried," Susan says, "they'll be fine."

She offers me coffee and the greatest blueberry muffins I have ever had. They're homemade, she tells me. Four are on the plate, and since she looks pretty thin, I'm counting on three of them for myself. If things don't work out with Dani, I am going to marry this woman, just for the muffins.

"So, you and Lisa Yates were coworkers at Ardmore Medical Systems?"

She nods. "Our cubicles were right next to each other."

"What did she do?"

"Same as me. We keep medical records up-to-date on our computer systems, which hospitals, doctors, and insurance companies can and do access."

"So nothing in the medical world is private?"

"It is, if you want it to be. But my guess is that you don't, and I would also bet that you signed away that privacy, probably without you knowing it."

"How did I do that?"

"On one of those forms at your doctor's office, or from your insurance company, that you didn't want to read. No one ever reads those things."

"Oh."

I ask her the standard questions about whether Lisa had any enemies, et cetera, but I get nowhere. She does not even know Gerald Kline; I get the feeling that the only thing close about her and Lisa was their cubicles.

Then I ask whether Lisa had seemed different lately, perhaps troubled.

"I don't know; I hadn't seen her since she quit."

"Quit? She quit her job?"

"Oh, yes. More than a month before she died. She didn't even tell me she was going to. I didn't even realize it until she didn't show up for a couple of days. I asked our boss, and he said she quit. He wouldn't go into why."

In the month before her death, Lisa broke up with Gerald Kline without telling her sister and quit her job without telling her best friend, Una Loge. This was a person who was dealing with significant things in her life.

"Do you have any guess as to why she quit?" I ask.

Susan shrugs. "Money? We're not exactly overpaid. But if you really want to get into the nitty-gritty of that place, talk to Don Crystal."

"Who is he?"

"He used to be one of our bosses, at least on the computer side. They fired him about a year ago."

"Why?"

She shrugs. "I'm assuming because he pissed off management. Don had a way of doing that; he can be a pretty unusual guy."

"So when you say he can tell me about the nitty-gritty, you mean the politics of the place?"

She nods. "I'll bet he knows where all the bodies are buried." Then, "Oh, that's a bad way to put it in this situation. I'm sorry."

I ask Susan a few more questions, which gives me an excuse to have the third muffin. Then I go into the other room to get Simon. He's lying on his back, and the two little dogs are trying to jump up to get on his stomach. Tamar, the Maltese, almost makes it, but just slides off each time. All three dogs seem to be enjoying themselves.

When we leave, I make a spur-of-the-moment decision to head down to the shore. Simon loved going in the ocean so much that I figure I'd give him another shot at it.

So we go back down to Asbury and spend almost an hour throwing and retrieving the tennis ball. Simon has a great time and so do I. I even take my shoes off; I take a cell phone photograph of my bare feet on the wet sand and email it to Dani. I'm a cop by training; I believe in presenting evidence.

We don't get home until about six thirty, after stopping for burgers along the way. We enter the house through the front door, and I immediately know something is wrong.

Someone has been in my house.

IT'S a cop thing.

I'm sensitive to something not being where it should be, something not being just right. It's an instinct that I have honed over time, but which I completely trust. The small rug in front of the front door has been moved slightly, and the corner is turned up. That's enough to confirm my feeling.

It could easily have happened by normal use, but I wasn't the one who normally used it like that. I'm certain of it. And even though I can't explain it, the place has a feel that it has been entered by someone that didn't belong.

My instincts do not include knowing whether the intruder is still present, so I draw my revolver and say, "Find the man, Simon. Find the man."

Simon perks up; the last thing he expected was to be going to work. He leads me to my bedroom, but if someone has been in here, they're gone. After that we search the house, methodically and carefully, but there is no one to be found.

I call my neighbors on either side of me, but they hadn't seen anyone near my house. After that I do a rough inventory; I don't have that much of value, but whatever I do have seems to be intact. I'm not surprised; this does not seem like a house burglary. People who do that don't make an effort to keep the interior neat and appearing untouched.

Whoever was here did not want me to know it.

With nothing obvious missing, my best guess is that the intruders were leaving a surveillance device of some kind, either audio or video. My experience in this is limited, but I search as best as I can for hidden devices, without coming up with anything. I have friends on the force who do this for a living, and I will get one to give the house a complete once-over.

I have a burglar alarm, but I rarely set it during the day, even though I know I should. I didn't expect to be gone that long; going down to Asbury Park with Simon was a spur-of-the-moment decision. That will teach me to be spontaneous.

For now there is nothing left to do. I'm not going to make any phone calls on my landline phone to anyone about it, for fear that the phone is tapped. I'm already sorry I called my neighbors, since anyone listening in on the calls would know I am aware that there was an intruder.

So I settle in to watch the Mets game. They're down three nothing in the sixth when the phone rings. I answer but don't say anything, and the caller says, "Douglas?"

I am good with voices and I can instantly identify this one as Kline's. "What do you want?"

"I have something to show you. It's about Lisa's death."

"What is it?"

"Come to my house; it's here."

"Tell me about it."

"You need to see it. Tonight. I can't sit on this. Tomorrow morning I'm going to the police."

"I'll be there in an hour. You'd better not be wasting my time, Kline."

"I'm not."

I hang up and consider the circumstances. I have absolutely no idea what he could have discovered that would be relevant to Lisa Yates's murder, but there's no sense trying to figure it out. If it exists, I'm going to see it soon.

I use my cell phone to call Laurie, who does not want me to go alone. "You could be walking into a setup, Corey. You have to realize that."

"I can handle anything this guy throws at me. Especially with Simon at my side."

"Really? Our operating premise is that this guy threw a professional hit man at Lisa Yates."

"Fair point. And there's another factor here." I tell Laurie about my feeling that an intruder was in my house today.

"I don't think you should go at all. He says he'll turn what he has over to the police? Let him do that."

"No, I'm going."

"Then let Marcus and me be there as backup."

"I'll tell you what. You can have Marcus in the area, close enough to move in if I call. I'll call him if I sense any problems. And Simon's a better problem senser than I am."

She reluctantly agrees, since she knows the final call on this is mine. "Marcus and I will both be there and ready. Call my phone for anything you need. Don't take any unnecessary risks."

"Okay. I'll be there in forty-five minutes." I hang up and turn to Simon. "Simon, old buddy, it's showtime."

We arrive at Kline's house exactly forty-five minutes from the time I got off the phone with Laurie. I don't bother calling to make sure that she and Marcus are in place; they are 100 percent reliable. And if anything had happened to delay them, Laurie would already have called me.

We pull up the driveway and park. Kline's car is there and lights are on in the house. Nothing seems amiss, though I'm not sure what amiss in this case would look like.

I decide to go in the back door without knocking, since Kline would expect me to go in the front. I'm not worried about the social niceties here; if any kind of unfriendly reception is waiting for me, I'm not going to make it easy on Kline and anyone he might have with him.

So Simon and I enter quietly into the laundry room. I take out my weapon just in case; I can always put it back if I don't need to use it. I can hear the television playing somewhere in the house; it sounds like the local news. They're giving the weather; local news consists of about 80 percent weather these days.

With my gun drawn and my trusty companion by my side, I walk slowly into the house. I head for the sound of the television; it would only be on for the amusement of humans. Who else would care about the frontal high keeping out the Canadian air? Especially since all one has to do is go out in the summer heat to know the Canadian air hasn't made it here.

But I don't hear those humans, and I hope they don't hear me.

I'm about halfway through the house when I turn into the den, which is where the television sounds are coming from. Kline is there, but he's unconcerned with the weather.

He's dead.

I am certain he's dead because the amount of blood around him approximates what would be found in an average slaughterhouse. Nevertheless, my cop training kicks in and I feel for a pulse just to be sure. I don't feel for it on his neck because he barely has a neck. That's where he was slashed.

I get some blood on the bottom of my sneakers; there is simply no way to avoid that. Once I determine that there is no pulse, Simon and I set out to make sure no one else is in the house. We do so slowly and methodically, but we turn up nothing and no one.

My first call is to 911 to report the murder. The operator professionally asks me the proper questions, then instructs me to remain on the scene, which I promise to do.

The next call is to Laurie to tell her what has happened. I say that since the police are on the way, she and Marcus can stand down. She seems hesitant, maybe thinking that I am being forced to make the call. I assure her that I'm fine, but my guess is that she and Marcus will hang around until they see the police cars pull up.

They don't have long to wait; the cops are here within five minutes, in force. They enter, guns drawn, and are immediately treated to the same gory scene that I uncovered. I have placed my weapon on the table, lest there be any confusion as to who might be dangerous.

"Holy shit," one of them says, but he's not the spokesman. The spokesman says, "What have we here? Who are you?"

"I'm the guy who called nine-one-one. My name is Corey Douglas, twenty-five years Paterson PD, K-9 division, recently retired."

He points to Simon. "This must be the K-9. He under control?"

"Totally."

"Against the wall. Assume the position."

I start to do so. "My weapon is on the table over there."

The cop frisks me and finds no additional weapons because there are none to be found. Then, "Take a seat over there. Hands where we can see them."

"You want to hear my story?"

"Not particularly. Homicide will be here in a minute; you can tell it to them."

His prediction proves accurate; Homicide does show up in al-most exactly a minute. The good news is that it is Lieutenant Robbie Lillard, who originally was Paterson PD. A lot of Paterson cops get started there and then move on to smaller towns in the adjacent area; they come in at a higher rank. Fortunately, I know Robbie pretty well from back in the day.

"Well, look who's here," Robbie says.

"How's it going, Robbie?"

"Well, I was home in bed twenty minutes ago, and now I'm standing in a goddamn butcher shop, so all in all, not that good."

I tell Robbie the whole story, starting with the domestic vio-lence, and moving on to Lisa's murder, leaving out nothing. He's most interested in why I was at the house tonight. "So he didn't tell you what he had to show you?"

"No. I pressed him, but he insisted I come here to see it in person."

"You have any idea what it was?"

"Honestly, none."

Robbie has me write out a full statement and sign it. When I'm done, I ask if he needs me for anything else.

He shakes his head. "No, you can get out of here."

Simon and I are happy to do just that.

I told Laurie that I want to take a day to think things through.

That's one of the advantages of working on a case without a client: there's nobody we have to answer to, and no timetable we need to adhere to. Among the negatives is that we're not getting paid.

Dani is getting home today and I'm going to surprise her by picking her up at the airport. Then we're going to do whatever she wants for the rest of the day. My hope is that she'll just want to go home and hang out. I'm a wild and crazy guy.

Dani looks genuinely happy to see me waiting for her at baggage claim, and I am rewarded with a much more than adequate hug and kiss. Once we're in the car, I say, "We can do whatever you'd like; the day is yours."

"Let's go home and hang out with Simon."

It's going to be tough to find a reason to end this relationship; I'm going to have to work long and hard at it.

But not today. Today we're going to hang out with Simon.

I never talk about work to Dani. I think it might be to protect her from an unpleasant world, but maybe it's because I don't think she will be interested. This time, though, when she brings up the subject, I open up and tell her everything.

"I'm sorry to lay this on you."

"Don't be; it's awful, but it's fascinating. The most interesting thing to happen to me in Miami was the caterer forgetting to bring the pot stickers to the farewell party." Then, "What are you going to do now?"

"I don't know. I've got two choices. I can drop the whole thing; my reason for getting involved in the first place no longer exists. I was going to nail Kline, but somebody else seems to have done that effectively.

"The other option is to continue investigating; if my goal was to find Lisa's killer, whoever it was, then there is certainly the real possibility that the same person killed Kline. I'm just not sure I have a role to play anymore; this seems like something the police can handle."

She nods and thinks about it for a moment. "Are you just bullshitting me, or yourself as well?"

"What are you talking about?"

"Look, I know nothing about your business; it's a world I don't understand and, on one level, don't want to understand. I'm way more comfortable dealing with pot stickers."

"I sense a *but* coming."

She smiles. "Here it comes. But . . . I know you; I know you really well. And I know that you may think you have to make a decision, but you've already made it."

I'm interested in what she has to say and, at the same time, amused by it. "So what's my decision?"

"You're going to keep investigating."

"And my reason?"

"Because you're a part of it. When Kline called you to come over, he made you a part of it. You pulled on a thread and now you have to watch the whole ball of yarn unravel."

"I like the ball of yarn metaphor."

She smiles. "I just made that up. Now, do you want to hear about the missing pot stickers?"

"No."

"Good. Take Simon for his walk and let's go to bed."

"Bed? It's only seven o'clock."

"I didn't say sleep, I said bed."

LAURIE, Marcus, Simon, and I convene at nine o'clock the next morning at Laurie's house.

Dani was right; after witnessing what I saw at Kline's house, there is no way that I can just let this go. Kline was reaching out to me, and he got killed before he could show me what he had. I don't owe it to him to follow through; but I do owe it to Lisa Yates, and to myself.

Laurie makes an entire boatload of pancakes and we plow through them. Andy and their son, Ricky, are there to help out, but as soon as Ricky finishes, he goes off to play video games.

I'm holding off talking about Kline until we finish eating, but I think Laurie and Marcus know what I'm going to say. I'm sure that in the same situation each of them would continue investigating, so they would expect nothing else from me.

The doorbell rings, setting off barking from Simon, Tara, and Sebastian. Andy goes to answer it, and a few minutes later he comes back into the kitchen. "Corey, you've got some visitors in the other room. Police visitors."

I go into the other room, expecting there to be more questions about last night. I am surprised they knew that I was here; maybe they reached Dani at my house and she told them.

The moment I walk in and see the cops, I know exactly what is happening. Robbie Lillard is there with three other cops, none of whom are smiling. If Robbie was just going to ask me some questions, he would not need this level of reinforcement.

I am going to be arrested.

"I'm sorry, Corey, but I am placing you under arrest for the murder of Gerald Kline." Robbie reads me my rights, a recitation I am not unfamiliar with. I notice that Laurie and Marcus have come in from the kitchen, and I feel a wave of embarrassment at them seeing me in this position.

"Corey, from this moment on, do not say one word. Not to anyone but me," Andy says.

"Who are you?" Robbie asks.

"His lawyer. I'm the one who is going to make you look ridiculous for making this arrest."

Within seconds I am being frisked and handcuffed. "Sorry about this, Corey," Robbie says again, and I believe him.

I'm taken to the county jail, where I'm processed and a mug shot is taken. The entire time I'm trying to not focus on the mechanics and the humiliation of this process, but rather why it is happening.

I was at the scene of a murder, and if Robbie did any investigating at all, he would have found out that I had a grudge against Kline. I came out and admitted it to Lieutenant Battersby, who was working the Lisa Yates murder.

But that would not be enough. I am not a career criminal with a history of violent crime; I am a former cop who has never been marred by a hint of scandal. They wouldn't have made this arrest, and especially so quickly, if they did not have more convincing evidence.

After a couple of hours in a cell, I am taken out and brought into a room where Andy Carpenter is waiting. Once we are alone, I say, "You know, I never hired you."

He nods. "Unfortunately, Laurie did."

"I can't pay your fee."

He nods again. "Even more unfortunately, Laurie waived it. Now can we move on to more important matters?"

"We can."

"You discovered the body and you had a grudge against the victim. We know they have that, but they have to have more."

He has just perfectly summarized my view. "I don't know what they could have because I didn't do it."

"Kline called you to the scene. If he did so under duress, then the purpose could have been to frame you. After he was forced to make the call, they killed him."

"They'd still have to have other evidence."

"Laurie said that someone broke into your house," Andy says.

A light goes on; I hadn't made the connection. "As far as I could tell, nothing was missing."

"Any idea why anyone would want to frame you for murder?"

"Not at the moment."

"Okay; we'll find out everything in discovery. I will see you at the arraignment tomorrow."

"Where is Simon?"

"At our house. We'll keep him until you get out; Tara insists on it."

"Will you get word to Dani about what's going on?"

"Laurie already did."

"What about bail?" I'm afraid of the answer.

"Tough in cases like this, but we'll do what we can. A lot will depend on which judge we draw."

"Maybe we'll get a judge who likes you."

"Maybe Amelia Earhart will be found singing karaoke at a bar in Fort Lee."

"Thanks for this, Andy." It'd be hard for him to say anything that would make me feel less anxious, but at the very least it's nice to know my team is in my corner. That's especially comforting since when I look across the ring to the other corner, I see the entire state of New Jersey.

Andy shrugs. "Any friend of Laurie's . . ."

I'VE attended a handful of arraignments in my career.

It was never in an official capacity because no testimony is offered at them. Mostly they were just cases where I was particularly and emotionally invested in an arrest I had made, and I wanted to see the accused handcuffed and facing justice.

This is different and weird; I am the one being arraigned. I am the one handcuffed, and I am the one facing what the system sees as justice. The only similarity is that I am emotionally invested.

Very emotionally invested.

Andy has gone over what to expect, even though we both know that I am aware of the procedures. All I have to do, when prompted, is to rise and say, "Not guilty." I don't need a teleprompter for that.

The prosecutor is Dylan Campbell, who I had some dealings with back in the day. He's smart and relentless, or at least that's how he seemed to me, and that's his reputation.

"Dylan hates me," Andy says. "I've beaten him three times, and I refer to him as Hamilton Burger." Andy is talking about the legendary Perry Mason prosecutor whose record compared unfavorably with the Washington Generals' record against the Harlem Globetrotters.

"Does he know you call him that?"

"I think so. I say it to his face."

"How does that affect me?"

"If he hates me, then he hates you. It's a principle of the law; the Latin name for it is *antagonis transferris*."

"Wonderful. Is there anyone in the legal system who doesn't hate you?"

Andy shakes his head. "Not since Laurie retired."

The judge is Nelson Wallace, which Andy considers relatively good news. He describes Wallace as fair and more willing to tolerate unconventional courtroom tactics than most judges. Andy's specialty is unconventional courtroom tactics.

Judge Wallace gavels in the proceedings, and Dylan presents the charges. There's some back-and-forth between Andy and the judge regarding pretrial motions and court procedures, but nothing that is particularly interesting to me. I am totally focused on the issue of bail.

Andy finally brings up the matter of bail, and Dylan immediately jumps up, obviously anticipating the request. "Your Honor, the State vigorously opposes bail in this case. The nature of the crime is so heinous, and the evidence so compelling, that public safety demands that the defendant be remanded to the county jail."

Andy shakes his head disapprovingly. "Your Honor, first of all, the evidence is always compelling to Mr. Campbell, yet based on my history with him, juries often seem to disagree. Secondly, though he has made a rush to judgment in the matter, he has not rushed to turn over discovery to the defense. But sight unseen, I can assure Your Honor that the evidence cannot be compelling, because Mr. Douglas is innocent.

"Mr. Douglas served as a police officer for twenty-five years and amassed an impeccable service record. During that time he was armed by the city and given the significant power that a badge carries, yet the public safety managed to have emerged unscathed. He protected the public; he did not endanger it."

"Mr. Douglas was never charged with murder during those years," Dylan says.

Andy nods. "Thank you for making my point for me. He was never charged with anything. Not once. Not ever. Not until this ludicrous charge was filed."

"What do you propose, Mr. Carpenter?" asks Judge Wallace.

"A substantial bail, the amount to obviously be set at your discretion. Also we would be comfortable with Mr. Douglas wearing a GPS monitor and staying within a seventy-five-mile radius of his home. He needs to be able to work; his obvious talent and experience make him an integral part of his own defense."

It looks like the judge is frowning a bit while Andy talks; I hope it's just gas. Finally, Wallace speaks: "Bail will be set at one million dollars. Defendant will wear a GPS monitor and will be limited to a fifty-mile radius."

He adjourns the session with a pounding of the gavel.

"One million dollars? It might as well be a billion," I say to Andy. "Can we negotiate it down to something I can afford?"

"Like what?"

"Five grand?"

"Seems unlikely. Let me see what I can do."

The bailiffs are on the way over to get me, so Andy gets up and says something to them, which I cannot hear. They pause in place as Andy goes over to the court clerk. He's there for less than five minutes and comes back.

"The bailiffs are going to take you in the back, and you'll get the GPS monitor."

"What happened with the bail?"

"I put it up."

"A million dollars?"

Andy shakes his head. "No, a hundred grand. Ten percent is all that's required."

"You shouldn't have done that."

"If I didn't, Laurie would have skinned me alive."

"You can never take credit for doing something nice for someone?"

He shrugs. "Not if I want to preserve my reputation."

DANI is waiting for me at my house when Andy drops me off.

We had spoken from the jail on the phone, but it was a quick conversation. I didn't call to tell her the result from the arraignment because I was heading directly home.

After a long, satisfying hug, she asks, "Did you get bail or did you escape? I'm fine either way, but if we're going to go on the run, I really need to get my hair cut first. And I'll need running shoes, and a fake mustache, and—"

I interrupt, "I made bail, but get your hair cut just in case I decide we should make a break for it."

"How much was your bail? I'm sorry if I'm being nosy, but that's a question I ask all my boyfriends."

"A million dollars."

"That's going to leave you a little strapped for cash, no?"

"Andy put up the ten percent."

"This is the same Andy who's working your case for nothing? The one you told me was a complete pain in the ass?"

"He has his moments. Come on."

"Where are we going?"

"To pick up Simon."

"You came for me before Simon? I'm truly flattered."

We don't talk much on the way to Laurie and Andy's, but I do ask, "Aren't you going to ask me if I did it? You know I couldn't stand Kline, and that I thought he was getting away with murder."

"Corey, if I was going to ask you if you did it, I wouldn't be here to ask you if you did it."

When we arrive, Laurie, Andy, Marcus, Sam Willis, Simon, Tara, and Sebastian are here to greet us. It's a welcome show of support, even if Sebastian is sound asleep. Nobody seems surprised that I've brought Dani along. They know her to be smart, and I also suspect that they think our relationship is further along than I am generally willing to admit.

The first thing I do, after I pet Simon, is ask Andy to come into the kitchen so I can talk to him alone. Once we get there, I say, "You know I've always considered you a pain in the ass."

"Come on, stop . . . I promised myself I wouldn't cry."

"Thank you for proving my point. But seriously, what you did today, what you are doing, is above and beyond. And you can't lay it off on Laurie. You are doing it, and I appreciate it."

"I'm happy to do it. Except for the part about actually doing it."

I know what he means; he's been unsuccessfully trying to retire from lawyering for a long time. "But we have to talk about money," I say. "And I don't mean the bail, because you're going to get that back."

"Good. Because if you skip bail, I will hunt you down if it takes me forever."

That draws a smile from me; Andy as a hunter of anything is a funny image. "You know what I mean; defenses are expensive, and I don't have that kind of money."

He frowns, as if annoyed and frustrated that we have to have this conversation. "Okay, here's the situation. I'm just going to say this once, so please refer back to it every time you consider bringing this up again. Laurie and I have more money than we will ever need. After this trial, if there is a trial, we will still have more money than we will ever need.

"You and Laurie are on the same team; you're friends. You and I are friends, in a can't-stand-each-other sort of way. She and I take friendship pretty seriously."

"But . . ."

"No buts. Every second you spend worrying about this is a second you're not spending clearing yourself. Much as I like to beat the hell out of Dylan Campbell, I want you and Laurie and Marcus and me . . . and Simon . . . to clear you before this gets into court."

"Fair enough. More than fair enough. But I thank you, and I owe you, big-time."

"One more thing. Since I am now your lawyer, and you are in legal jeopardy, our relationship has changed."

"What does that mean?"

"It means you need to listen to my wise counsel, so as to prevent you from making your situation worse."

"I understand."

"Good. Are we done here?"

"We're done here."

We go into the other room to discuss our strategy. "I've been thinking about the situation, which may not come as a surprise," I say. "But I think there are certain assumptions we can make. One is that whoever was behind the murder of Lisa Yates was also behind the murder of Gerald Kline."

"What makes you so sure of that?" Laurie asks.

"Don't misunderstand; I'm not saying that Kline was not involved in the Yates killing. I would not be the least surprised if he was. But there is someone else, above Kline on whatever totem pole we're dealing with, who is pulling the strings.

"The next assumption is that my confronting Kline at his house the other night ultimately led to his death. Not just because it followed so quickly, but more because of their so far successful attempt at framing me. I said something which worried Kline, and which in turn must have worried his bosses. So they got rid of both problems, by killing Kline and framing me."

"Which means it was not a domestic dispute, or a broken relationship, that caused this," Andy says. "You may have originally thought that's what you were dealing with, but you stumbled into something much bigger. And there is big money involved."

"Why do you say that?" Laurie asks.

I jump in. "Because someone hired the person who killed Lisa Yates. Maybe it was the twenty-five grand in cash that Kline took out, or maybe not. But either way it didn't come cheap. And I would think there is a good chance that Kline's killer was hired as well. Could very well have been the same person."

"I'm going to offer a third assumption," Laurie says. "I don't believe that there was anything Kline was going to show you that night. I think he was either forced to say that or was a willing participant, not realizing it was going to result in his death. He may have thought he was setting you up to be killed, Corey."

"I agree," I say. "So where do we go from here?"

Laurie turns to Marcus, who has not said a word. "Marcus, can you try to find out who was hired to kill Lisa Yates?"

"Yunhh." I assume that means yes because Marcus nods when he says it.

"How will you do that?" I ask.

Marcus just shrugs, so Laurie picks up the slack. "Marcus knows people in that world. He has a knack for getting information from those people. If the guy is local, we have a chance. If he was brought in, it's less likely."

"I have an idea," Sam Willis says, the first time he has talked as well. He says it a little sheepishly, as if not sure he should be speaking up.

"That's what you're here for," Laurie says.

He nods. "Okay. We monitored Kline's phone after you left that night, and he didn't make any calls for the next twenty-four hours. Yet it seems obvious that he spoke to someone about you."

"Right," I say. "But they could have met in person."

"That's possible," Sam says. "But maybe he called on a different phone, one we don't know about. Maybe one that isn't even in his name."

"So?"

"So virtually every phone has a GPS in it. The phone company can tell you where a specific phone is at a specific time."

"How does that help us?" Andy asks.

"It can also be cross-checked to reveal what phones are in a specific location. If Kline had a different phone in that house, I believe I can tell you the number, by cross-checking the GPS data."

"And if they met in person?" Laurie asks.

"If it was at Kline's house, then I can tell you what phone his visitor was using. And if it was elsewhere, I can follow Kline's phone and tell you where he was."

Laurie turns to me. "Corey?"

She's asking me the question because she knows about my reluctance to let Sam use "extralegal" methods. The issue is whether I will feel differently now that it's my ass on the line.

"Sounds like a plan," I say.

Dani smiles. "That's my little hypocrite."

THERE is not a huge amount of publicity about my arrest.

It obviously made the local papers; the coverage has been greater than it would have been had I not been an ex-cop.

But as far as I can tell, it hasn't hit the TV local news. That is a function of geography: since Paterson is under the New York television umbrella, it rarely makes the cut as to what goes on the air. If the media were to cover every murder that happens in the New York metropolitan area, it would be all murder, all the time. There would be no room for weather, and no one would know where the hell the Canadian air is, or what is preventing it from getting here.

I don't care that much about the publicity either way, though it's not fun to be thought of as a slasher/killer. I realize that people naturally assume that someone who is arrested is guilty; I used to have that impression myself. But I feel confident that I will be vindicated, and my reputation restored.

But the publicity level, or lack of it, does have some independent importance. In the investigation we are going to conduct, I am going to want to talk to a lot of people, some of them friends or colleagues of Kline's. If they think of me as his killer, it could prove to be a definite conversation stopper.

We are still figuring out who to approach, while waiting for Marcus and Sam to come back to us with information. In most situations I am incapable of just sitting around, but with a GPS bracelet on my ankle I am particularly anxious. No, *anxious* is not strong enough . . . *crazed* would be the proper description.

I open my computer and start to get some information off the internet. I'm not sure what I'm looking for, and I'm certainly no Sam Willis, but it gives me something to do.

I google Lisa Yates and read the stories covering her murder. There's nothing there that I don't already know. Biographical information on her is short, but her Facebook page is at least partially enlightening. Apparently Facebook pages stay up after a person dies, which I guess makes sense, since there is no one to take it down. I'm sure Facebook has no interest in monitoring death records; they only make money off the living.

I switch to googling Gerald Kline. Reading the media stories about his murder is painful, especially the follow-up stories that identify me as having been arrested for the murder.

The worrisome part, as these stories remind me, is that the police and prosecutor felt confident enough to make the arrest. I get it that I had a grudge against Kline and was foolishly vocal about it. That known bias, coupled with my being present at the scene and calling the police, should have made me a suspect. Maybe I should even have been a prime suspect, although I would have thought my long record on the force would have given them pause.

One thing they did not do is pause.

Andy pointed out, and there is no doubt he is correct, that they have other evidence they consider compelling. I am worried about what it could be because the people we are up against seem to be smart and well financed. They could well have done something to set me up.

My mind is obviously wandering, so I force myself back to the internet. Kline is said to have run seminars that often led to people being hired into the medical services industry, which was his specialty. He was also a headhunter in the industry, which was obviously why his seminars would be well attended. For Kline, one of his jobs fed off the other.

Kline's company is called Healthcare Recruitment and Marketing Services. It's not exactly a catchy name, but the website makes up for it with glitz and cool graphics.

There are three people in the company, or at least there were three before Kline departed the scene. The cofounder is Stephanie Downes, and if her smiling photograph is current and not photoshopped, then she is probably in her late thirties and quite attractive.

The third person in the firm, listed as an executive assistant, is Carol Ayers. Ayers looks a good ten years older than Stephanie and considerably less attractive, but they do have the wide smile in common.

I click on seminars and see that one is scheduled for today at noon at the Woodcliff Lake Hilton. It is to be conducted by Stephanie Downes, and tickets, priced at seventy-five dollars, can be purchased online or at the door.

I would have thought that Kline's death would have put the company's operations on a temporary hold, and maybe the cancellation just happens not to be on the website. On the other hand, they might be going ahead with it, and I have nothing else to do, so my GPS bracelet and I are off to Woodcliff Lake.

I get to the hotel at eleven forty-five and spend ten minutes navigating the parking lot, looking for a spot. I can't tell how many of the cars are owned by guests of the hotel or attendees of the seminar; if it's the latter, then the sponsors are doing well.

I follow the signs to the ballroom, which is where the seminar is being held. A table is set up outside the room, and two women sit behind it with small metal boxes, I assume to hold cash. They also have credit card machines.

"I'm not too late, am I?" I ask.

One of the women smiles at me; I recognize her as Carol Ayers, the executive assistant listed on the website. "No, sir, they're just starting now."

"I'll pay cash," I say, and hand her the seventy-five bucks.

"Thank you. Please fill out this questionnaire before going in."

"Why?"

"So we'll have your information on file."

"You know, it's the strangest thing, but I don't want my information on file."

Not waiting to debate the point, I open the door and enter the ballroom. It takes about thirty seconds for my weird mind-counter to determine that seventy-nine people are in attendance, not including the woman onstage, Stephanie Downes.

Speaking into a handheld microphone, she says, "So I looked at him and said, 'You're the doctor?'" This gets a large laugh from the attentive audience, so I assume that whatever she said before rendered the line funny.

Then she turns serious. "But the larger point, which I suspect many of you understand or you wouldn't be here, is that the medical services industry is only going to get bigger. As we live longer, we develop more and more medical issues." Then she smiles. "I'm starting to feel it when I try and get out of bed in the morning."

Another laugh from the audience; Downes has them eating out of her aging hand.

I stay for a half hour. Downes lectures the audience on how they can prepare to enter the medical services industry, and how they can make themselves palatable to prospective employers. It seems like boilerplate stuff, but she gets away with it because she is charming, and probably because the audience thinks she can help them get in the door.

I'm on the way home when my cell phone rings. Caller ID says it is Laurie's home number, and when I answer, Andy is on the phone. "Where are you?"

"Heading home from Woodcliff Lake."

He doesn't bother to ask why I was there. "Stop over here. We got some of the discovery."

"Is there a problem?"

"There is definitely a problem. We'll talk when you get here." Click.

ANDY, Laurie, and I go into the den as soon as I arrive.

I am not looking forward to what I am about to hear; clearly whatever the prosecution has is a serious negative for our case.

Andy gets right to the point. "The police searched the entire block around Kline's house. Four houses down, the people had a Dumpster back near their garage. In it the police found a plastic bag with bloody clothing in it, a sweatshirt, sweatpants, and sneakers. It was a Rutgers sweatshirt. There was also a bloody kitchen knife."

I know where this is going. "The break-in at my house."

"They had no trouble getting a DNA match; apparently you sweat when you wear a sweatshirt and sweatpants. So their obvious theory is that the reason you did not have blood on you is because you were smart enough to bring a change of clothing with you. It's the kind of thing a cop would think of. I assume you didn't report the break-in?"

"No; I had no way to prove that it really happened; it was just an instinct I had by the way the carpet was slightly out of place. But more it was a feeling I had. And there was nothing missing."

"Except the clothing," Laurie points out.

"I have a bunch of hooks on the inside of my closet door. I hang sweatpants and sweatshirts on those hooks; there are always three or four of each. There is no way I would have noticed one set missing; it would never have entered my mind that they would be stolen. And I probably have five pairs of sneakers on the closet floor."

"This certainly explains the quick arrest," Andy says.

"What do we do now, Counselor?"

"We deal with it. We've known all along that they had something that caused them to move so quickly, and now we know what it is. Our job hasn't changed; we need to figure out who is behind this and why."

"Okay. I've seen my share of frame-ups; it's just particularly disconcerting that it's happening to me."

Laurie nods her understanding. "We'll get where we need to go."

"I spent a half hour at a seminar this afternoon. Gerald Kline's partner ran it; her name is Stephanie Downes. She is apparently not mourning in seclusion."

"What did you learn?"

"How to apply for a job in the medical services industry, and that it's a huge help to have computer skills."

"Well, now we're getting somewhere," Andy says. "What made you go there?"

"Because Gerald Kline met Lisa Yates at one of these seminars, and he may well have placed her in a job. That connection could be important, and this could somehow be tied to their work."

"They didn't work at the same company," Laurie says. "He

just got her hired there. I'm not saying we discount it, but we have no indication their work life was even connected after that."

"They had a romantic relationship, and who knows what else," Andy says. "For all we know they were selling bazookas and hand grenades in their spare time."

They are both right, but my instinct says otherwise. "Don't forget that Lisa Yates quit her job not long before she was killed. Her coworkers were surprised by it and she apparently never gave anyone a reason. That could be significant."

Andy nods. "Yes, it could be."

"One thing we know for sure is that they were somehow linked, and I don't mean just romantically. And whatever it was killed them both."

"It was something they knew that made them dangerous," Laurie says. "That's where you came in, Corey."

"What do you mean?"

"When you showed up at Kline's the first time, it signaled that you were digging into his life. But you were looking at him for Lisa Yates's murder, based on the domestic violence incident."

I nod. "Which must be why he almost seemed relieved; it was because I wasn't looking into something else."

Laurie nods too. "But you must have said something which spooked him, or more likely spooked whoever he was working for. Think carefully, did you say anything that could have set them worrying?"

I think for a while and then it hits me. "I told him I knew about the cash he withdrew."

"Bingo," Andy says.

VIRTUALLY everyone has someone they report to.

It's simply a fact of life; just a handful of people are technically at the top. But even most of them have someone overseeing them, be it a board of directors, or shareholders, or "the American people."

The man who called himself Carlos was certainly not the exception to the rule. He was very much aware of that and literally called his boss "boss." It didn't matter; Carlos knew that names meant nothing with these people.

Carlos had a good amount of autonomy in his job. He had talents that his boss admittedly lacked, and up to this point Carlos had used good judgment in utilizing them.

He did not for a second believe that he was not always in competition for his job. Months ago his boss made a slight slip of the tongue that seemed to reveal that the operation included other people on Carlos's level, perhaps in different areas of the country. Carlos knew that he could be moved out if the boss so desired.

So far the boss had not so desired, but Carlos was also certain that his boss was not alone at the top either. He would occasionally allude to some colleagues that he would consult with.

Carlos thought this conversation was going to be relatively pleasant. He believed that he had simultaneously solved two problems successfully: Kline was permanently out of the picture, and the ex-cop, Corey Douglas, was effectively eliminated. The damage, if any real damage was done at all, was completely contained.

The boss had a different view: "You've made matters worse. Kline was never a real threat; he had too much invested in this. And the cop cared only about the domestic violence garbage. Now he knows it had nothing to do with that, and we have a lawyer and more investigators trying to get him off. And there will be a public trial analyzing every piece of it."

Carlos was taken aback and worried. "It's manageable."

"Everything is manageable; it is just now infinitely more difficult."

"I'll come up with an effective strategy; I always do. You know that."

"I do not know that; this incident is the very definition of a bungled approach. You will clear any future steps with me before you take any action."

"If that's what you want . . ."

"That's what I want."

"MY name is Corey Douglas. I'm a private investigator. I'd like to speak to Ms. Downes about a personal matter."

"Just a moment, Mr. Douglas."

This is me taking a wild shot; I would be very surprised if Stephanie Downes is willing to see me. If she doesn't recognize my name, then she'll say no because she wouldn't want to take a meeting with a stranger about an unspecified topic. If she recognizes my name, then there's that little problem about her thinking I killed her partner.

It takes about sixty seconds, and I'm surprised when Stephanie Downes's voice comes on the line; I'm good at voices and I recognize it from the seminar. "Good morning, Mr. Douglas. I understand you left the seminar early. Was it something I said?"

"How did you know I was there?"

"My assistant recognized your face; she was also Gerald Kline's assistant, so she has an interest in media coverage of his death. And she surreptitiously photographed you as you were leaving, just to be sure."

"Sounds like a terrific assistant; you should hang on to her. So can we talk?"

"I believe that's what we're doing now."

"I meant in person."

It takes about thirty seconds for her to respond; at first I'm not sure if she has silently hung up. Then, "I suppose so. It will be one of life's adventures."

"Where would you like to have this adventure?"

"Someplace public; I'm curious, but not crazy. Do you know the Suburban Diner on Route Seventeen?"

"I do. I ate there last week."

"Shall we say three o'clock? That way it won't be too noisy, but will still be public."

"Perfect. See you then. You can recognize me from the picture your assistant took."

Dani, Simon, and I go for a late lunch at a favorite place of ours in Ridgefield Park, where we can eat outdoors. We take two cars, so she can take Simon home and I can go on to the Suburban Diner.

We eat at an outside table in deference to the ridiculous rule that Simon cannot eat indoors. He's a lot cleaner and neater than quite a few people I know, me included. To reduce his embarrassment, we order him a plate of grilled vegetables and a bowl of water.

At three o'clock, having eaten a lovely lunch and then sent Dani and Simon home, I enter the Suburban Diner and don't see Stephanie Downes anywhere. I take a table near the back and hope that she hasn't decided this was a bad idea.

At three fifteen she comes in, sees me, and walks to the table.

"You look just like your picture." She sits down. "Did you also take a good mug shot?"

"I forgot to smile."

"Don't you hate when that happens?"

This is a self-confident woman, comfortable bantering with a man she thinks slashed her partner's throat. Or maybe she's just nuts.

She signals a waitress and orders coffee and a fruit plate; I opt for just coffee. Once the coffee is served, she says, "You have the floor."

"I'm trying to discover who killed Gerald Kline."

"I was under the impression that that crime was solved."

"I'm under a different impression, so humor me. I'm not expecting you to tell me it was Mr. Plum in the library, though I'm fine if you do. I just want to understand how Kline lived, who he associated with, that kind of thing."

"I know much less than you'd expect." Apparently she's willing to keep talking to me.

"He was your partner for how many years?"

"The very premise of your question is incorrect. We shared a business and both of our names were on the masthead, but we were not partners, not in the traditional sense. At least not for a while."

"Elaboration would be good, and appreciated."

She takes a sip of coffee and settles into her story. "We were both in this business, starting out on our own. This is going back a while now. We were competitors, of a sort, and decided to join forces. It made sense economically, and together we controlled much of the market, so we got an enhanced reputation. But within our company we kept separate accounts. Each of us made what we earned, and we shared the common expenses. It worked well, at least until you or some other person put a gruesome end to it."

"What happens to his clients now?"

"Hopefully I'll get my share." Then, "Aha, a motive to kill. Is that what you think?"

I shake my head. "No. It's a worthy motive, but it doesn't fit. Because whoever killed Kline likely killed Lisa Yates."

"Lisa. That was a shame."

"You knew her? Then is there any chance you killed them both? If you'd confess, it would make my job a lot easier."

"Sorry; can't help you there. I met her a few times at industry events; she was with Gerald. Seemed lovely, which is why they seemed mismatched."

"You didn't like Gerald?"

"I did not. He had a way about him, a charisma, which one needs in this industry. You saw me demonstrate it onstage, I suspect. But while he could turn on the charm at will, his veneer was thinner than most, and he was a very disagreeable man.

"But you seem like an agreeable man . . . for a murderer." Again, she has no reason to trust me, but she certainly isn't acting like I might actually be a murderer.

"You're making me blush," I say.

"YOU want the good news, or the better news?"

Sam Willis is asking the question, and I have to say I like the way he phrased it. He's called a meeting to tell us what he's found and asked for the entire team, including Andy, to be present. Sam seems to like an audience.

The meeting did not start well. Before Sam showed up, Laurie and Marcus told us that Marcus has been unable to identify the shooter of Lisa Yates. Considering Marcus's connections and power of persuasion, that is a significant disappointment and a surprise to Laurie.

Everybody, including me, is of the belief that big money must have been paid, big enough to have the shooter keep his mouth shut. Or perhaps he is afraid of his employer and thinks that an indiscretion could either be dangerous or an impediment to future employment. Or perhaps he was brought in from out of town.

We're guessing a lot here.

But now Sam has arrived, and his opening salvo is promising. Andy answers his question by saying, "Just tell us everything, Sam. The order is not important."

Sam nods. "Okay, the good news is that I have identified three cell phones that were in Kline's house within a couple of hours of the time he was killed. Four, if we count yours, Corey. One of the other three belonged to Kline; it was registered in his name. A second one, an unregistered burner phone, probably also belonged to Kline. According to GPS data, it was most recently at Ridgewood police headquarters, probably confiscated for their investigation.

"So the last phone is the interesting one, since it may well have been brought there by the killer. That phone is registered to Alvin Szabo, address on Grand Avenue in Englewood. That's Szabo, *S-z-a-b-o*. But the name is fake, and the address listed is actually a gas station."

"So how do we find him?" Laurie asks.

"We don't have to," I say. "We find the phone."

"That's right, but with a slight correction," Sam says. "We've already found the phone. It lives in a high-rise apartment in Edgewater. But there's no Alvin Szabo at that address, so we have no way of knowing where in the building the phone is. GPS measures location, but not height. So we have to follow the phone when it moves."

"You can do that?" I ask.

"Yes. I'll tell you where the phone goes, and when, and you can do what you'd like with it. But I haven't told you the better news yet."

"Sam, I like your style," Andy says.

"I had a hunch, so I went back to check out the recent history on the phone GPS, and it paid off. That same phone was in the area when Lisa Yates was shot."

It's significant news, but not surprising. We've thought all along that the same people, if not the same killer, were behind both murders. This is confirmation of that, but more significant is that we might be able to get our hands on the killer.

"Okay, team, what's your next step?" Andy asks.

"We identify him, then follow him and see where he leads us," Laurie says.

I shake my head. "We can try that, but he's not likely to lead us anywhere. We have nowhere close to a guarantee that he meets in person with his employer, and that employment may be over anyway. He's done what he was hired to do."

"So what would you do?" Andy asks.

Andy is taking an interesting approach here, different from that in other cases we've worked with him. When we're working on behalf of one of his clients, he solicits and respects opinions, but he calls the moves and he sets the strategy. In this case, with me as the client, he is deferring more. He recognizes that it's my ass that is on the line; if I'm going to go down, he wants me to have taken my best shot.

"We confront him," I say. "I'm not saying he'll confess, or that he'll reveal his employer, but it might shake things up. And if we have his phone information, maybe he'll use it and we can track who he calls."

"Marcus?" Laurie asks.

Marcus doesn't bother saying anything; he just points to me and nods. I'll take that as a ringing endorsement.

"Okay," Laurie says. "Sam, can you monitor the movements? Work with Marcus, so we can identify him, follow him, and figure out the best time to approach. Once we do, Marcus and I can move in."

"Excuse me?" I ask. "You think I'm not going to be a part of this?"

"That's exactly what I think," she says. Then, "Andy, you want to explain this to him?"

Andy picks up the baton. "You can't be there, Corey. If something goes wrong and violence ensues, your GPS monitor will place you at the scene. You'll be back in jail for the duration. And I don't have to tell you that this is the kind of event at which violence can definitely ensue."

"I'm not happy about this," I say.

Laurie smiles, but her words are serious. "Get over it."

FIVE days have gone by since Sam identified the phone.

He and Marcus have been giving us periodic reports, and while I am going insane over the wait, they have actually been making good progress.

It took less than a day to locate the man who went by the name of Alvin Szabo. Sam Willis identified an individual as the man carrying the phone when he left the apartment building, and Marcus took a photograph of him.

Andy sent the photo to Pete Stanton, the captain in charge of Homicide for the Paterson Police Department, who is a close friend of Andy's. Both Laurie and I also know Pete well, but it seemed best that Andy approach him.

According to Andy, when Pete heard that he could help me by finding out who the man was, Pete was eager to do it. It turned out that it didn't take much effort; Pete was very familiar with him.

According to Pete, the man's name is Jake Gardener. Gardener is well-known in homicide circles as an extremely dangerous man who, while no doubt responsible for many deaths, has avoided even being charged, much less convicted. He does his job well, works alone, and does not come cheap.

Once we located Gardener, Marcus became the key player. It has been up to him to decide the best time and place to deal with Gardener, which meant Marcus had to monitor the man's movements and habits. Marcus has been doing that for three days, going on four.

It feels like two months, going on a year. Though Dani won't admit it, I've got to be driving her nuts. Even Simon doesn't want to go for a walk with me.

Finally, the call comes from Laurie. "Come on over; time to go over the final plans."

When I get there, Marcus and Andy are there as well as Laurie. She gets right to the crux of the matter. "Gardener likes baseball. And he appears to be a Mets fan."

"What's his favorite color?" I ask obnoxiously.

She ignores me, as she should. "The reason his devotion to the Mets is important is because he goes to the same restaurant every night, which is where he watches the game. There's a TV over the bar. We don't know what he does when the Mets aren't playing, but that doesn't matter because they're playing tonight.

"They're in St. Louis playing the Cardinals so the game will start just after eight Eastern. A normal game would end at eleven thirty or so, and Gardener has been sticking it out to the end. Last night, for example, the Mets lost by eight runs, but he watched until the final pitch."

"DeGrom and Wainwright are pitching," Andy says. He knows that I am aware that those pitchers mean it will likely be a low-scoring game, and therefore quicker than most.

"When it ends, he leaves," Laurie says. "By that time the place is just about empty; Marcus thinks they might even keep it open that late because Gardener wants them to. Maybe they're afraid of him, or maybe he's a big tipper; either way it doesn't matter to us."

"So you grab him when he leaves the bar?" Andy asks.

"Not quite. He parks in a lot about a block and a half from the bar, near the back where there aren't many cars. He drives a souped-up Mustang, and it's possible he doesn't want to take a chance on it getting scuffed up. That works in our favor; it's dark back there."

I nod. "As Clemenza put it, there shouldn't be 'any pain-in-the-ass innocent bystanders' around."

"Right. So we wait by his car," Laurie says. "When he gets there, we surprise him."

"I wish there was something I could do," I say.

"There is. You can watch the Mets game and text me when it's over."

"Hell, I can do that," Andy says. "Let's talk about how careful you guys are going to be. Pete said that Gardener is dangerous as hell."

"Marcus," Laurie says, which usually effectively ends the discussion.

"Let's not be overconfident," Andy says. It must be a weird feeling for him to be sending his wife off on this mission, even though she is a competent ex-cop who can handle herself extremely well.

"I agree," I say. "If you run into any difficulty, just abort."

"Marcus, can we do this?" Laurie asks.

"Yunhh."

Once again, Marcus has the last grunt.

LAURIE and Marcus took up their position behind Gardener's car at ten fifty.

Corey reported that the game was already in the eighth inning. He said something about Andy being right about deGrom and Wainwright, but that was more information than she needed.

The game wound up going ten innings and didn't end until just after eleven thirty. That was unfortunate in that it caused Laurie and Marcus to have to wait, but fortunate in that it made it even less likely that other people would be around.

Finally, Corey texted and said the game had ended. It took ten minutes from that point for Gardener to approach his car. By that time Laurie was standing there waiting for him. He didn't see her until he was almost at the car, because of the darkness.

"Hi, I've been waiting for you," Laurie said, making her voice friendly rather than threatening.

"Yeah?" Gardener said, wary but intrigued, just before Marcus body-slammed him into the car, causing his head to put a dent in his Mustang and defeating the purpose of his parking back there. With a practiced maneuver, Marcus quickly frisked him and removed a handgun from his pocket.

Marcus turned him around, and he took a couple of steps away from the car, perhaps contemplating fighting back. But he seemed dazed and ended up just standing there.

Laurie stood to his left and Marcus to his right. They had done this maneuver before; they considered it disorienting to the person they were questioning. Laurie held a handgun on him; Marcus just stood there being Marcus.

"You killed Gerald Kline and Lisa Yates," she said.

"Who the hell are you?"

"You killed Gerald Kline and Lisa Yates," she repeated.

"And you two are next. You signed your death certificate tonight."

"Wow, you're scary. Either that or you're a cowardly worm who shoots women from cars."

Marcus had not done anything or moved a muscle; he was just watching Gardener intently, waiting for any possible move.

"I won't be shooting you from a car. I'll be doing it close up."

"Who paid you to kill those people?"

Gardener just laughed. "I did it for the fun of it. And no one is going to have to pay me to kill you two."

Just then there was the sound of a car horn, loud and startling in the otherwise silent night. Laurie made the mistake of looking in that direction, dropping her guard momentarily.

Gardener moved with incredible speed, whirling around and coming toward her. Marcus saw it immediately; there was the glint of a blade, which had been hidden in Gardener's wrist.

He brought it toward the throat of the stunned Laurie and was less than six inches away when his head was crushed by

Marcus's forearm and elbow. Marcus followed up with a second blow as he was going down, but it was thoroughly unnecessary.

Heads are not built to absorb that kind of force; planets are not built to absorb that kind of force. Gardener was dead well before he hit the ground.

Laurie recovered quickly, felt for a pulse on Gardener's neck, and realized that the next few minutes would be crucial, as they decided what to do. Her cop training told her to call 911, wait there, and tell the police what had happened. What Marcus did was a defensive act, pure and simple. He was saving her life.

But that might not be how it would look to the arriving officers. It might look like they had lain in wait and ambushed Gardener, killing him when he resisted. Marcus could wind up being arrested.

Marcus seemed to understand the situation and had already decided what they had to do. He mentally went through the areas they might have touched while waiting for Gardener, and he wiped away any chance of fingerprints.

Laurie watched him do it and weighed the issues in her head. This was no small decision for her; all her training said to call the police. But her common sense said otherwise, and her allegiance to Marcus did as well, so she realized they had to leave.

Which they did.

Gardener stayed behind and waited to be discovered in the morning.

"LEAVING was not our only option," Laurie says. "I'm not sure we did the right thing."

She has been relating the night's events ever since she and Marcus came back to the house. I was home while it was going on but came to Laurie and Andy's when Laurie texted me the simple words "It's over."

That had sounded ominous to me, and based on the story I just heard, *ominous* doesn't even cover it.

"There was nothing else you could do," Andy says.

Laurie shakes her head. "The law says otherwise. Legally we were supposed to stay there, report it, and tell the story of what happened. We killed a man."

"And what would you have accomplished?" Andy asks. "The legal system, which as you know I would like to exit, abhors a vacuum. They wouldn't have shown up and said, 'Oh, you guys killed him? No problem. You can go home; give our best to Andy.' They would have started an investigation, and it would go on forever. And there would be no way of predicting how it would wind up."

"He was a murderer. I'm an ex-cop; the presumption would have been with us."

"He was a murderer? Who says so? The justice system? Then why wasn't he ever convicted? Why wasn't he ever even charged? Everyone in this room knows he was a murderer, he basically admitted it to you and even tried to demonstrate it on your neck. But according to the justice system, he was pure as the driven snow."

Laurie is obviously getting frustrated by the conversation. "Look, I'm not necessarily disagreeing with you; nor is Marcus. We're the ones who walked away. But there's a moral issue here also."

Time for me to speak up. "No, there isn't. He tried to kill you. Marcus clearly acted in your self-defense. And he was a killer; the justice system may not know it, but facts are facts. He was a killer.

"I'm troubled by the legal side of this as much as you, Laurie . . . maybe more. But at the end of the day, there was no good option. I think I would have done what you did, but I can't say for sure. I wasn't there; you and Marcus were. It was what it was, and you did what you did. Let's move on."

Laurie frowns. "This is going to bother me for a while."

I am frustrated too, but for different reasons. "Laurie, we have some real-world evidence that you did the only thing you could do. You think calling the police would have worked out just fine? I'm with Andy on this, and you know why? Because I did the right thing: I called the police when I found Gerald Kline's body.

And I'm walking around with a damn GPS bracelet on my ankle because of it.

"And you know what else? I had to spend my last million dollars on bail."

Everybody laughs at this, including Andy and Laurie, who put up the money. Actually, Marcus doesn't laugh because he wasn't born with the laugh gene. The laughter takes a lot of tension out of the room.

The truth is that I don't know what I would have done had it been me instead of Laurie. The Kline analogy doesn't apply because I didn't kill him; I only found his body. Marcus did kill Gardener, so his legal position would have been more perilous than mine, had I not been framed.

I also don't know if my spoken view that Laurie did the right thing is how I really feel. It certainly must be colored by the fact that I'm the one we're all working to help; I have a huge self-interest in this.

Laurie and Marcus were in that position because of me; I feel guilty and responsible for having put them in harm's way in the first place. I owe them a debt that I can never repay. And speaking of pay, they are professional investigators who are not getting a dime for this.

So I am grateful to them and I am going to support them. What I would have done is and will remain a hypothetical, and I'm not going to worry about it. One thing Andy was certainly right about is that my GPS bracelet and I should not have been there; if I was shown to be on the scene, it would have been a disaster.

But that's now behind us. Laurie was right when she texted me the message "It's over."

"We need to talk about our next steps," Andy says. "Gardener, to state the obvious, is now a dead end."

"Can we discuss it tomorrow?" Laurie asks.

Andy looks at his watch. "It's already tomorrow."

"I know," Laurie says, "and I'm tired. Marcus and I have had a bit of a rough night."

"I agree," I say. "Tune in tomorrow."

"YOU know I hang on your every word of wisdom, right?"

Pete Stanton was calling Andy at eight thirty in the morning as Andy had just returned from walking Tara and Sebastian. Knowing what the call had to be about, Andy took it on the speakerphone so Laurie could hear what was said.

"I know you do, Pete. That's why I share it with you. On your own you're not exactly the brightest bulb in the chandelier."

"And you impart so much of that wisdom because you never seem to manage to shut up. Looking back, I particularly remember the time you told me that when it comes to criminal investigations, there is no such thing as a coincidence. I have found that to be so true."

"You going to get to the point anytime soon?" Andy smiled at Laurie since they both knew exactly where Pete was going. Laurie was somewhat less amused; she was still shaken up and doubting her decision to leave the scene.

"Sure. You sent me a picture of Jake Gardener and asked who he was. I told you. I didn't ask why you wanted to know because I basically didn't give a shit. So last night the same Jake Gardener winds up dead, hit in the head by either Aaron Judge swinging a baseball bat as hard as he can, or Marcus."

"Wow, a young guy like that, cut down in the prime of life . . . it really puts things into perspective. Here's another piece of wisdom, Pete. Live every day to the fullest because you never know."

"Yeah. But, you see, now I do give a shit about your interest in Gardener because he was killed right here in Paterson, the same city in which I am captain in charge of the Homicide Division. You understand?"

"I do, and I admire your dedication. I have full confidence you will solve the crime, despite your track record. Now, are we done here?"

"We will be done when you tell me what happened to Jake Gardener."

"Pete, have I ever lied to you?"

"Constantly."

"And I regret that, deeply. But this time I'm going to tell you the truth. I don't have the slightest idea what happened to Jake Gardener." Laurie cringed at the obvious lie, but didn't say anything. "And I'm sure that Marcus, if you could understand a word he said, would tell you the same thing."

"Maybe you'd like to tell it to me under questioning down here at the precinct."

"It would be my pleasure. I should have said this the last time I was down there, but I love what you've done with the place."

"This is not a game, Andy. A human being . . . I will admit, a piece-of-garbage human being . . . was killed last night. I am going to get to the bottom of it. So if you have any information, and I have no doubt that you do, you need to share it with me."

"Okay; point taken. I will tell you what I know, and it is all that I know. However, I will not tell you how I know it; that is privileged."

"Are you going to tell me before I'm too old to deal with it?"

"Here goes. Jake Gardener killed Lisa Yates and Gerald Kline. He was paid a large sum of money to do it, but I do not know the source of that money. When I do know, you will be the first person I share it with. Well, maybe not the first, but in the first or second tier."

"So you're telling me that Gardener is the real killer in a murder case for which your client has been accused. There's another one of those coincidences."

"Maybe I was wrong that there's no such thing as a coincidence. I'm wise, but I'm not infallible."

"ANDY Carpenter and associate to see Jason Musgrove."

"Does your associate have a name?" the receptionist asks.

"That's his name: Harry Associate. Don't feel bad, everybody makes that mistake. Harry's used to it."

The receptionist just frowns and picks up the phone, telling someone that Andy Carpenter and associate are here to see Jason Musgrove. As I've previously mentioned, I've always considered Andy a pain in the ass; but when he's doing it on my behalf, he doesn't seem quite as irritating.

Moments later a young woman who could be the receptionist's twin sister comes out to lead us back into the executive offices of Ardmore Medical Systems. They have the top eight floors of a modern Paramus office building off Route 17, and based on the expensive furnishings and appointments, medicals systems are good systems to be involved in.

Jason Musgrove, since he's the Ardmore CEO, is in the

legendary corner office, with glass walls overlooking the high-way. I guess this is as good a view as one could have if you're on a highway, since the other side sort of has to be your parking lot.

I checked out Musgrove before we got here. He's only thirty-eight, but looks older in person because he's clearly losing the battle of the bald. He's got an MBA from Stanford, so it is likely he is not a dummy, or at least he's smarter than me. Until recently I thought Stanford was a city in Connecticut.

Musgrove is peering down at his glass desk, pretending to work as we come in. Only three sheets of paper and a phone are on his desk, but he's devouring them. It's a technique I've seen before; feigning being weighted down with work gives him an excuse to rush the meeting to a quick conclusion.

"Mr. Musgrove . . . ," the young woman says, causing him to look up as if he's surprised to be interrupted.

He says, "Mr. Carpenter?"—then notices there are two of us. That look of surprise is quickly replaced by a look of greater surprise when he recognizes me. He composes himself. "You brought your client."

"I did," Andy says.

"I agreed to meet with you alone."

"Actually, it never came up. But you are welcome to have someone else join us if you feel outnumbered."

"I could also call this off right now."

"And as I mentioned, the alternative is to undergo a pretrial deposition, for which you should bring all business and personal records. And Mr. Douglas would be in the room for that as well. So if you'll just bear with us for a few minutes, it shouldn't be too painful. I promise to protect you if Mr. Douglas seems inclined to get violent."

Musgrove frowns. "Let's get this over with."

Andy and I agreed that I would not contribute to the interview unless I saw something important that he was missing. So he starts it off.

"Great. What exactly do you do?"

"Me or my company?"

"Your company."

"Medical information comes in to us, we catalog it, preserve it in our computers. Then we supply it to medical providers and insurance companies who require it. That's the simple version."

"Whose information?"

"Almost everyone's. Even yours, I would bet."

"Don't I have to authorize that?" Andy asks.

"Of course. But you very likely did when you visited your doctor. It was a lengthy form. It's unlikely you read it, more likely it was summarized for you."

"Why would I sign?"

"To take a drastic example, let's say you are allergic to a number of drugs. You are in Ohio on business, and you get in a car accident. You arrive at the hospital unconscious. They are going to administer drugs; wouldn't it be nice if they had your list of allergies?

"Or you want medical or life insurance. Do you want to have to round up your records by calling all your doctors and then sitting for an invasive physical, or would you like the insurance company to easily access the information?"

"Do you have competitors?"

"Not really. Other companies do what we do, but they are spread out geographically. We handle most of the East Coast; this is our home office, but we have five satellites. It's a bit of an anachronism; computers make geography relatively meaningless, yet that's how our industry is organized. We have working relationships with the other companies."

"What was your working relationship with Gerald Kline?"

"He was a headhunter for us. If we had an opening, he rec-ommended candidates. We interviewed them, and if we agreed with his assessment, we hired them."

"Was he the only person you used?"

"Yes. We hire people on our own through HR; but for the higher-level jobs, we used Gerald's services. He was very good at it."

"What were the talents necessary for the higher-level jobs?"

"Reliability, experience, computer expertise is essential . . ."

"What will you do with Kline out of the picture?"

"When I make that decision, you'll be the first to know."

I thought I would find it annoying not to be asking at least some of the questions, but Andy is covering the ground quite well.

"How well did you know Kline personally?"

"I would say moderately well. We had lunch quite a few times, and maybe three or four dinners. Most of the time we talked about work, but that wasn't all."

"Did you talk about Lisa Yates?"

"Some. He and Lisa were together for a while."

"Did it bother you that he was in a relationship with one of the employees he recommended?"

Musgrove shakes his head. "No. First of all, their relationship began well after she came here. And second, it's not like he was her boss; they had nothing to do with each other in their work life."

"Any idea who might have viewed Kline as an enemy?"

Musgrove looks at me. "Present company excepted?" Then, "No; I was quite shocked when I heard the news." He looks at his watch. "Are we done here?"

Andy nods. "I believe we are."

IT would be overstating it to say that Jason Musgrove was worried.

At most, it could be said that he had some concern. Not because there was any real danger, but rather because things had gone so smoothly for so long that even a slight glitch assumed a greater importance.

The ex-cop and his lawyer had said nothing in the meeting to indicate they had the slightest idea what was going on. They asked questions about Gerald Kline because they were trying to find his killer. That made perfect sense given that the ex-cop was going to be put on trial for the crime.

But Musgrove would alert his team, so that they could then be on the lookout for any developments that might be worrisome. They were thorough and had immense resources and abilities, and Musgrove could count on them to be extra careful. There was too much at stake, and they had waited too long, to take any other approach.

Musgrove was in charge of the operation, but he had ceded much of it to his associates. Part of it was because they were so good at what they did, but the truth was that Musgrove set it up this way with an eye to the future.

When it was over, the others would disappear, never to be found again. That was how they wanted it, and they were capable of making it happen. Musgrove, on the other hand, wanted to remain behind, living the life he had built.

At times Musgrove felt uneasy about his having given the team too much power, too much leverage over him. But there was no way around it, and he was not truly worried.

When the time came, Musgrove believed he could handle any and all eventualities.

IN my view the Crown Inn is not an inn. It's a motel.

Inns are places that are old and quaint and have two faucets in each sink, one for the hot and one for the cold. They don't have televisions in rooms, but they do have stairs that creak, and four or five thousand antique shops within a mile radius. They serve good muffins and coffee in the morning, but you have to sit at a large table and make conversation with the other guests.

Motels are two-level buildings that look run-down about an hour after they are built. You can park your car in front of your room. There are vending machines on each floor, but no place to get change to use them, and no way to effectively complain if the bag of M&M's doesn't actually fall into the bottom tray. They have televisions, but no guide to tell you the channels. The soap is the size of a saltine, and their carpets are bought already pre-worn.

I may be generalizing here.

By any standard other than its name, the Crown Inn in East Rutherford is a motel. It's also the place that Sam Willis said Lisa Yates paid for with a credit card during the last month of her life. Lisa's house on Derrom Avenue was nice; this place would not seem up to her standards.

I'm not sure that there is anything to be learned here, but I'm positive that there's nothing to be learned by sitting home. I'm certainly curious as to why Lisa would stay in this place; my best guess is that she was hiding. Unfortunately, I'm not likely to learn who she was hiding from by talking to the staff at the Crown Inn.

I walk into the small office out front and ask the blank-faced teenage boy behind the desk to get the manager.

"He's not here."

"You have got to be kidding," I lie. "He said he'd be here."

"I don't know what to tell you."

"I don't have time for this." I look at my watch to demonstrate my focus on time. "I'm here to get Lisa Yates's things."

"Who is she?"

I feign increased annoyance, leaning toward anger. "Who is she? Is this your first goddamn day? She was here for a month and then had to leave town. She sent me to get her stuff. Look it up."

He sits up straighter. "Okay . . . okay . . ." He looks her up on the computer and says, "Here she is. She owes two weeks' rent."

"I know. I already had this damn conversation with the manager. Now how much does she owe, I'll pay it. Then you take me to her room, I'll get her stuff, and get out of this dump."

He looks at the computer again. "Three hundred forty dollars."

"What a damn rip-off," I say, but I count out the cash and give it to him. Maybe I can fill out an expense form and get Andy to reimburse me. "Let's go."

He gets the key and takes me to her room and opens it. "See you later," I say at the open door, to make sure he leaves.

I go inside. Gathering her stuff is pretty easy; there are two suitcases, still closed and filled. There are no clothes in the closet or the drawers, no toiletries in the bathroom, nothing to show that she stayed here. Actually, it's obvious that there is no way that she did stay here; I'd bet she was keeping this room as a potential place to hide. At least that's how I see it.

I take the two suitcases, make one more check to see that nothing else is in the room, and leave. I walk around to my car, which is near the motel entrance, and load them into the trunk.

Obviously the police never became aware that Lisa was renting the room or they would have come and confiscated her stuff. I suppose at some point it could come back to haunt me that my GPS monitor will show that I was here, but I'll deal with that when the time comes.

In the meantime, I head home to look through the stuff I've just stolen.

"YOU moving in, or moving out?" Dani asks, when she sees me come in with the suitcases.

"I stole these from Lisa Yates's motel room."

"You know, it's possible that you're a career criminal."

"And a damn good one." I bring her up-to-date on the circumstances behind my theft.

"What are you hoping to find?"

"A clue, maybe. I have no idea. You want to help me look through all of this? In case there's female stuff I shouldn't see?"

"Sure; I certainly wouldn't want you to see female stuff. But if I help, will that make me an accomplice?"

"Absolutely."

"Can I be a sidekick instead? I've always wanted to be a sidekick."

"I can't think of a better sidekick to have." I point to the suitcases. "You take that one and I'll take this one."

We open both of them on the living room floor; they seem to be filled with clothing. I take the items out of my assigned bag, and at the bottom there is a toiletry case. I open it, but there doesn't seem to be anything unusual in it.

"Just clothing and stuff in here," I say.

"Same here." But Dani's going through her bag more slowly than I am. "Wait a minute. . . ."

"What is it?"

"An envelope." She takes out an eight-and-a half-by-eleven-inch manila envelope, which looks thin. If anything is inside, it couldn't be more than a few sheets of paper. She hands it to me to open, which I do, being careful not to tear anything inside.

It is, in fact, three sheets of paper. They are three newspaper obituaries, which appear to be printed from the internet. I look through them quickly, and they seem not to be out of the ordinary in any way.

One is for a Mr. Samuel Devers, 71, of Springfield, Massachusetts. Another is Ms. Doris Landry, 73, of Somers Point, New Jersey. The third is Mr. Eric Seaver of Brunswick, Maine. The dates that they died are listed and are all about seven weeks ago. These three people died within five days of each other.

The obituaries themselves are boilerplate; they don't do much more than announce the deaths. There are no mentions of planned services, though in two cases the families recommend donations to specific disease charities in lieu of flowers. I assume those are the diseases they died of.

In two cases the people are survived by their spouses; Ms. Landry is survived by her son, Steven.

I call Andy and tell him what I've done and about the discovery of the obituaries. I tell him I'll scan and email them to Laurie, and he says that Dani should do it on her computer, in case the authorities issue a subpoena to go through my emails.

Andy puts Laurie on the phone, and I suggest that she give this information to Sam, to see what he can find out about the three deceased people. "The obituaries were hidden at the bottom of a suitcase. They weren't there by accident."

When I get off the phone, I ask Dani to scan and send them to Laurie.

"No problem," she says. "That's the kind of stuff that side-kicks do."

"I just don't see anything unusual about these people. They basically lived normal, uncontroversial lives."

Sam has done a quick background check on the three deceased people whose obituaries Lisa had in her suitcase. I was hoping he'd come up with some case-breaking clue, but he obviously has not.

"Did they have anything in common?" I ask.

"Well, they've all kicked off, so there's that. And while I don't want to speak ill of the dead, none of them seem to have made much of an impact on the world. They lived pretty long lives, and then sayonara."

"That's beautiful, Sam," Laurie says. "You have the heart of a poet. No criminal records for any of them?"

"No. Not so much as an unpaid traffic ticket. I'm getting copies of the death certificates, so maybe you'll see something unusual in them."

"Any of them wealthy?"

He shakes his head. "Nothing out of the ordinary."

I try again. "So no reason to think that Lisa Yates had a relationship with any of them?"

Sam shrugs. "I can't really say that. I can say that there is no obvious connection that exists online. But I can dive a lot deeper; I just did a surface search. They could have been pen pals for all I know."

Sam's comment gives me an idea. "Can we get access to Lisa Yates's emails? Maybe she communicated with them that way."

"Do you have her computer? Or phone?"

"No and no. I assume the police have them."

"Can you get me her email address? If not, I'm sure I can get it. So the answer to your original question is yes."

"I'm sure I can get her email address from her sister. I was going to contact her anyway."

"Okay, let me know when you have it, and I'll get her emails. Last three months good enough?"

"Plenty good enough."

When I get home, I call Denise Yates, Lisa's sister. "Sorry to bother you. I'm calling to ask you a few more questions, and to see how you are doing."

She sounds tired. "Getting by. One day at a time; isn't that how you're supposed to do it?"

"So I'm told. I'm lucky that I haven't had to go through something so awful." I'm a bit relieved; if Denise is aware that I have recently been charged with murder, she isn't acting like it.

"I hope you don't have to. Any progress on the case?"

"Some, but that's what I wanted to ask you about. Do these names mean anything to you, and do you know if Lisa had any connection to them? Samuel Devers, of Springfield, Massachusetts; Doris Landry, of Somers Point, New Jersey; and Eric Seaver of Brunswick, Maine."

She thinks for a few moments. "Not off the top of my head. Can you tell me them again? I want to write them down. Maybe something will come to me."

I tell her the names again, and I assume she's writing them down. "I also wanted to ask you for Lisa's email address."

"That's one I can answer. She had two; one for personal and one for work."

She gives me the addresses and I thank her. "I'll be in touch when I come up with something."

I get off the phone frustrated that we can't yet find a connection between Lisa Yates and the three people in the obituaries. Their deaths were in some way meaningful to her. They all died shortly before Lisa rented the motel room in what looks like a plan to hide, if she needed to run.

She packed bags to keep there, and those obituaries did not print and pack themselves. She did both, and she wouldn't have done those things without a reason. That motel room was going to be her safe place, where she felt she could hide and not be harmed. She wanted those three pieces of paper with her.

I just wish I knew why.

MY father, if he was alive, would have described Don Crystal as a "character."

Most people of my father's generation would have said it as a negative, but not him. If he encountered someone like Crystal, he would have been sort of bewildered and sort of amused, but he wouldn't have been critical. He was a live-and-let-live guy, even if he couldn't identify with certain offbeat kinds of "living."

Crystal certainly has an interesting look about him. His hair is long; if it were combed down, it would probably not reach his shoulders, but would come pretty close. But that is a moot point; his hair does not look like it's been combed or brushed since the Mets last won a World Series.

When I get to his house, he greets me at the front door in pajamas . . . with feet on them. They're not bunny feet, so that's a plus. But I haven't seen an adult in pajama feet in a while; it takes a major effort not to stare.

He lives in what seems like a fairly large, and quite old, house in Tenafly. When I walk in from the front door directly into the den, I am struck that, besides a couch, there is no other furniture at all. No chairs, tables, television, nothing. I can't speak to what might be in the bedroom or kitchen, or in what I assume are quite a few other rooms, judging from the outside, but I've got a hunch that this house is not home to many book- or bridge-club gatherings.

Crystal practically jumped at the chance to talk to me when I called him. All he had to hear was that I wanted to talk about Ardmore Medical Systems, and I thought he was going to send a limo to my house to bring me here. That he referred to Ardmore as "that cesspool" leads me to believe his assessment is not going to be all positive.

When I interviewed Susan Redick at Ardmore about Lisa and her work there, Susan had said that if I talked to Don Crystal, I'd learn about the "nitty-gritty" of the place. Based on this house, I definitely think she was right about at least the "gritty" part.

"You want something to drink?" Crystal asks. "I've got water and Tang."

"Tang? The stuff the astronauts used to drink?"

He nods. "They probably still do; it's good stuff."

"I didn't know that it was still around."

He gives me a look. "Oh, sure. You just have to know where to find it."

I decline the Tang, and he sits on the couch. I sit on the arm of the couch farthest from him; it seems to be the cleanest available spot. I tell him I'm looking into the death of Lisa Yates.

"She's dead?"

"Yes, murdered in a drive-by shooting."

"Wow. I don't spend much time with the mainstream media. The kind of things I read, unless there was a wild conspiracy theory about her, or she was killed by aliens, I wouldn't have seen it."

"How long did you work at Ardmore?"

"Way too long."

"Can you quantify that?"

He smiles. "Man, I can quantify everything; I'm a living, breathing quantifier. I was there for four and a half years."

"Why did you leave?"

"They padlocked my office and had security lead me out. It made me feel unwanted."

"Mind if I ask why they fired you?"

"Let's just say I was not management friendly. I would call them assholes when they were making stupid decisions, and they made a lot of those. So who killed Lisa?"

"That's what I'm trying to find out. Can you think of anyone at Ardmore that would have had a reason to hurt her?"

"Nah, she was a nice lady. Smiled at me every morning; I can't say that for everybody there."

"Was she good at her job?"

"Hey, it wasn't brain surgery, you know? Brain surgery isn't even brain surgery, you know?"

I don't know that, but I think it's best to ignore the weird utterances coming from his mouth and try to get him to focus.

"She worked on a computer, inputting stuff, that kind of thing. Management thought the people who did that were all Steve Jobses. Hell, Steve Jobs wasn't Steve Jobs, you know?"

"Your work was in computers?"

"Yeah, if you call setting up their whole damn system being in computers. And if you call handling all their IT stuff for four and a half years being in computers. Then, yeah, my work was in computers."

"Who replaced you?"

"Nobody. At least nobody who knows anything. They brought in a guy named Miller, or Marler, or Marley, or some asshole."

I'm floundering here, trying to get past his bitterness and into something meaningful to me.

"Did you know Gerald Kline?"

"Gerald Kline . . . Gerald Kline . . . oh, right . . . he's the guy they used to pick some of the geniuses they hired. Never met him, never wanted to. What about him?"

"He was killed as well."

"No shit? Who killed him? Same person that killed Lisa? Man, all the weird stuff started happening after I left."

"What are you doing now?"

"Living off the money they paid me to leave. Where do you think I got the cash to buy the Tang?"

He starts laughing at his own joke, which I have to admit seems funny in the moment.

"If I ask you to think about Lisa Yates and Gerald Kline and call me if anything comes to mind, will you do that?"

"No chance." He laughs again. "I'll be too busy looking for work; my Tang money is starting to run out. Maybe one of your old friends in the police department wants to hire a computer guy? I interview really well; I'll even buy new pajamas."

"That should do the trick."

WHAT is the world record for most consecutive unproductive indoor meetings?

Whatever it is, we must be approaching it. We keep getting together at Laurie and Andy's house to discuss positive developments and strategy. What we come away with is that there are no positive developments, and we obviously need to come up with a new strategy.

Only Sam Willis seems to be getting anywhere, and he's the one who called this meeting. Sam promises that this time he's hit the mother lode, which is probably one of the better "lodes" to hit.

I just hope he's right; my trial is bearing down on us.

"So, Corey, you made the suggestion that I should check Lisa's emails. I did and found something very interesting. It's an email from Lisa to Doris Landry . . . do you remember that name?"

"Of course. She's the woman from Somers Point. Her obituary was one of the printed articles in Lisa's suitcase."

"Right. I think you'll find the content very interesting, and I'll show it to you in a second. But just as interesting is what is not there. It seems to be the last email in a fairly long chain. . . . There were eight previous emails. All are shown in this one email . . . one on top of the other . . . nothing unusual about that. But all the previous emails are gone; Lisa erased them and then emptied the trash. I can only assume she screwed up and forgot to erase this last one. Or maybe that's just the way she kept her emails organized."

He takes a small folder out of his briefcase and hands four pieces of paper to each of us. They have been collated and stapled; Sam is efficient.

We all start reading. It is, as Sam described it, an email chain between Lisa Yates and Doris Landry. They are clearly comfortable and familiar with each other; there are occasional references to family and things that each of them has been experiencing. Doris, for example, says that her son, Steven, is coming that day to take her out to dinner.

Then, on page three, comes the bombshell. Landry asks a question, phrased with deliberate vagueness, as if concerned someone else might wind up reading it: "I'm afraid to ask. But is there anything new with your situation?"

After Lisa says that she hadn't wanted to bring it up for fear of "unloading" her problems on Landry, Lisa does just that: "It's getting worse. Gerald doesn't think that Rico will do anything. I think he's crazy. . . . Rico doesn't just dispense this stuff for nothing. He's a dangerous guy; he's connected to people. I'm afraid to leave my house."

"Are you still going to quit your job?" Landry asks.

"I think so. I can't live here anymore. If I go somewhere else and get clean, I can start all over. Without Gerald."

Landry responded, "You can do it, Lisa. You have strength you don't even realize."

Lisa's answer, and the last words on the chain, were "I'm going to need it."

Andy is the first one to speak after we've all read it. "Well, this qualifies as a surprising development." He is obviously and deliberately understating the case.

"Lisa and Kline were buying drugs," Laurie says. "Do we know if the autopsy report said there were drugs in Lisa's system? Or Kline's?"

"We have Kline's autopsy report in the discovery," Andy says. "I don't recall any mention of drugs, but I'll look at it again. We don't have Lisa's report because Corey isn't charged with her murder."

"I can access a copy," Sam says, and I don't think anyone doubts that he can.

"This still leaves a lot of unanswered questions," I say. "For one, who the hell is Rico? For another, while it demonstrates a connection between Doris Landry and Lisa, why was Lisa carrying around her obituary?"

"I've got a third," Laurie says. "Why would Rico bother to frame you for the Kline killing? He didn't find it necessary to frame anyone for Lisa's death. Framing someone doesn't seem like a drug dealer's style. And how would he know about you?"

"I can't answer those questions, but it does explain Kline's cashing those checks. He was buying drugs. Apparently it was not enough money to get him off the hook. And for more than twenty grand, it was a very large hook."

"Marcus, can you try and figure out who Rico is?" Laurie asks. "I'm assuming he is local."

"Yunhhh."

"I'll also ask some people in the department. I doubt Rico operates completely under the radar."

Andy takes out his copies of the obituaries and looks at the one for Doris Landry. "It says she's survived by a son, Steven. We need to talk to him."

"I'm feeling like there are pieces to the puzzle that are still missing," I say. "For instance, Jake Gardener was a high-priced hit man. Is that the kind of guy drug dealers hire? Doesn't feel right."

I can see Laurie react with a slight frown that she quickly covers up. Gardener's death is still bothering her; she believes that she and Marcus should have called the police that night and reported what happened. I have tried to convince her otherwise, but she comes from the same cop culture as I do, so I understand her feelings.

"Maybe Gardener was also a customer of Rico's," Laurie says. "He could have been paying his tab by killing Lisa and Kline."

"Maybe," I say. "But it's also possible, and I agree this would be a coincidence, but just because Lisa was afraid of this Rico guy doesn't mean he was the one that had her killed. If she and Kline were operating in this kind of world, they could have made other enemies."

"Speaking legally, this is an enormous plus whether Rico is the killer or not," Andy says. "If we can show that Lisa and Kline were taking drugs and in fear for her life from a dealer, it would be pretty hard for the jury not to find reasonable doubt about your guilt."

"I want more than reasonable doubt," I say. "I want complete exoneration."

"A noble goal. But as your lawyer, I'll settle for you not spending the rest of your life in prison."

I'm uncomfortable with a lot of this, but I probably shouldn't be. Lisa clearly expressed a fear of a drug dealer in this email, which opens up a promising area of investigation.

Andy's right; from the standpoint of our defense, we've struck gold. Maybe we'll find Rico and he'll break down and confess, and the judge will take off my GPS bracelet, apologize profusely, and all will be right with the world.

Maybe.

JASON Musgrove, the man who was called "boss," was as much amused as worried.

On one hand, they were up against an apparently competent adversary. And that adversary was certainly tenacious; Carlos had stupidly ensured that by framing this Corey Douglas guy for Kline's murder.

That was a monumental error; by placing Douglas's future freedom in jeopardy, it ensured that he and his colleagues would be relentless in discovering the truth. That Carlos had made such a dumb mistake caused Musgrove to question his choice of Carlos for the position he held.

One more mistake like that and the position would be temporary. Musgrove's team would see to that. That team was incredibly talented; each one was extraordinary in his own right.

But Musgrove had created it all, had the access and the ideas. But he was a worrier because the operation had gotten so big, and so violent, that he did not feel fully in control of the nuts and bolts of the operation. He was aware that he did not fully know how foolproof and impenetrable the construction of the system was.

Musgrove's amusement with the current situation came from his team's ability to manipulate his enemies and the entire situation. His people knew everything the other side knew, and more important, what they thought they knew.

He knew that they had discovered the obituaries and was certain that they had no idea of the significance of them. They would go down one dead-end road after another, until Douglas was in jail, and Musgrove's team would be left with more money than they could ever spend.

But just in case, he would continue to watch them.

He and his team were always watching.

WE just caught another break.

Somers Point, New Jersey, where Doris Landry lived and died, is well outside the radius that I am allowed to travel from my GPS prison. So I was not going to be able to go down there to interview her surviving son, Steven. Andy and Laurie were planning to drive down to do that.

Sam got a phone number for Steven, and Andy called him to ask if they could visit. It turns out that he does not live down there at all, but in Freehold, which is much closer.

He was quite willing to talk to us about his mother, even though Andy was vague about the reason for the request. To make matters even more convenient, Steven said he was planning on traveling to Manhattan the next day, to handle some personal business and to deal with a few issues in his mother's estate.

Steven said that he would be willing to talk to us there, if we'd make the trip in for an early-morning meeting. So that is what Andy and I are now doing. We're meeting at Sarabeth's, a terrific breakfast place on Amsterdam Avenue on the Upper West Side, near where Steven said his meetings are.

We get there twenty minutes early, which is lucky, because Andy considers it a badge of honor to find a parking spot on the street. He says it's because the parking lots are so absurdly expensive, but I don't think that's what it's about. I think he relishes the challenge.

We finally find one, and when we arrive at the restaurant, a man in his forties is sitting at a table set up for three. He brightens when he sees us and waves us over. "Andy Carpenter, right? I recognize you from television. I'm a big fan; I admire what you do."

Andy has made a number of TV appearances in connection with high-profile cases he's worked on, but he's not exactly mobbed by paparazzi when he walks down the street. That Steven Landry recognizes him does qualify him as a fan.

Andy smiles with as much modesty as he can, but doesn't bother to introduce me. Steven doesn't seem to mind or notice; his total focus is on Andy. If an ex-cop comes to breakfast and no one acknowledges him, does he make a sound?

We order breakfast, followed by some meaningless chitchat between them about New York traffic and Freehold Raceway. Steven says he lives just a few blocks away from the track, and Andy claims to have misspent his youth there. Less than fascinating stuff, but the pancakes are terrific.

"Small world," Steven says, and Andy and I both nod in agreement.

"So, what could my mother have to do with Andy Carpenter?" Steven finally asks, continuing to pretend as if I am not here. I'm starting to wish I wasn't here.

"We're interested in learning about a friendship your mother had with a woman named Lisa Yates."

Steven doesn't hesitate. "Oh, sure, Lisa. Mom mentioned her a lot. She really liked her."

"Do you know how they met?" Andy asks.

"Hmmm . . . I think it was on a cruise. Mom took a bunch of them after Dad died; she wanted me to go, but come on, a cruise with your mother?"

"You're sure it was a cruise?" I ask, just to show I'm awake and present. Steven answers me, but continues to look at Andy. Maybe if I punch Steven in the face, he'll notice me; at least it's something to consider.

"Actually, I'm not. But I do know Mom liked Lisa a lot. I think she felt sorry for her as well; she described her as 'troubled' a few times."

"Troubled how?" Andy asks.

"I don't know; if she said, I don't remember. But Mom saw herself as a healer; not a faith healer or anything weird like that, but she thought she could help people by talking to them, and by just being understanding. Mom was really good like that; she liked people and people liked her." Steven shakes his head sadly. "I miss her every day. My dad too."

"But no mention of anything specific?"

Steven thinks for a little while. "I think she might have said that Lisa fell in with the wrong guy. But honestly, I could be wrong about that too. Mom had a lot of friends, and she seemed to attract needy people. She believed everyone had good in them; it was just hard to let it come to the surface and stay there."

"Your mother sounds like a good person," I say.

He nods. "She really was. I thought she'd be lonely once Dad died, but she kept up these friendships. I kept in touch as much as I could, but we all have lives, you know? And then one day it's too late."

"Were a lot of her friendships through email?" Andy asks.

Steven laughs. "Oh, yes. Mom really latched on to emailing. She was old-fashioned about a lot of things, but when it came to emailing, she was one of those early adopters."

"Were you able to notify all of those people when she died?"

He nods. "Every one of them. Took a while, and a lot of them wanted to talk, share memories, that kind of thing."

"Was Lisa Yates one of the people you notified?" I ask.

He hesitates for a second. "I'm sure she must have been. There were so many I can't remember. And some of them I just knew their email addresses, not even their full names."

"That must have been some job," Andy says. "I guess you just searched through her emails and replied to the most recent one from each person?"

Steven nods. "Yup. Took most of a day."

We've run out of questions at the same time we've run out of pancakes, which is a happy coincidence. We thank Steven for his time and head for the car. Luckily it hasn't been stolen off the street and sent to a chop shop while we were at breakfast.

Once we're on the West Side Highway heading home, Andy asks my impression of Steven and the interview.

"Seemed like a friendly, nice guy. And I think he was lying through his teeth."

"You're not as dumb as you look."

"So you thought he was lying also?"

Andy nods. "Except for the part about how much he admires me."

I'M shocked that Andy also thought Steven Landry was lying.

First of all, Steven was pretty good at it. He came across as friendly, helpful, and sincere, at least on the surface. And Andy gave no indication that he disbelieved him. I hope that I didn't either.

"What made you distrust him?"

Andy shakes his head. "You first."

"Okay. The guy's mother just died, and this famous criminal attorney—"

"That would be me, in case you're scoring at home."

"—this famous criminal attorney, Andy Carpenter, who he has on this pedestal for some bizarre reason, starts asking him questions about a relationship his mother had. Not once does he so much as hint at any curiosity as to why said famous criminal attorney is asking the questions."

"He could have been awed by me."

"As are we all. But the part that got me was his story about how he notified all his mother's friends that she died by returning their most recent emails."

Andy nods his agreement, so I continue, "First of all, how did he even get into her computer or phone, and then if he did, how did he get her password?"

"Maybe she had a standard one that she always used. A dog's name, something like that. Go on."

"Do you use *T-A-R-A*?"

He frowns. "Damn, now I have to change it."

"I didn't buy it that he knew her passwords, but it's possible. But then he painstakingly returned the most recent email for all these friendships she supposedly had? People he didn't even know? That's what published obituaries are for."

Andy nods again. "Right. And the Lisa Yates thing bothered me. He remembered her right away when we asked, but didn't remember returning her email? The one in which she said she was afraid for her life from a drug dealer? And we didn't see his email to her on the pages Sam gave us. The guy was playing us. Although the part about admiring me and being a fan did ring true."

When we get to Andy's house, we update Laurie on our conversation with Steven Landry. She asks the obvious question: "Why would he lie?"

"Could have been to make himself look good," I say. "The caring son, involved in his mother's life to the point where he contacted all of her friends on her passing. It's possible that the last time he saw her was twelve years ago this Tuesday; don't forget, they lived nowhere near each other."

Andy nods in agreement. "Also could be that, under questioning by a famous lawyer for whom he has such admiration, he didn't want to admit that he knew about Lisa's drug issues and her fear of being murdered. He might feel bad or embarrassed that he didn't come forward in a manner that could have saved her life."

"Okay," Laurie says. "All good points. Now come up with a scenario in which he lied for a reason that relates to our case. What could the death of Doris Landry have to do with the murder of Lisa Yates?"

Unfortunately, that question leaves me stumped and seems to have the same effect on Andy. The truth is that it's possible Steven Landry was basically telling the truth, albeit with a little starstruck embellishment. Maybe it's even probable.

But if Andy and I are right and he actually was lying, I have no idea how it could have anything to do with Lisa Yates's death. And it's another giant step removed from the murder of Gerald Kline, which is the charge I am facing.

Andy responds to Laurie by saying, "Why do you have to ruin everything with your logical questions? It's a very unattractive trait."

Laurie smiles. "Sorry about that." She says that she'll have Sam check out Steven Landry, but I think she's doing it more to humor us than anything else.

"As long as you're doing that, why don't we ask Sam to get Lisa Yates's phone records for the last few months?" I ask. "It would be interesting to know if she talked to Doris Landry, or for that matter the two other people whose obits she had. And while we're at it, he should get Kline's phone records as well."

I've become increasingly comfortable with using Sam to hack into computer systems in ways that are somewhat less than legal. That's what facing life in prison can do to a person.

"Will do," Laurie says. "And in the meantime, here's what I suggest. We take the information you learned from Steven Landry, including and especially the fact that you think he was lying, and file it away. Hopefully, as we investigate further, it will click into place and make sense."

The "investigate further" part is a bit of a problem. I have another person to talk to at Ardmore, but I am running out of "furthers" to investigate.

"Well, then let me help you with that," Laurie says. "While you and Andy were off having a lovely all-boys breakfast, Marcus and I were actually getting things done."

"Meaning?"

"Meaning I think we've found Rico."

"How?" Andy asks.

"I asked Gerry Kimbrell; he's a DEA agent I once worked with on a case. He wasn't familiar with Rico, but asked around and came up with Rico Barnes, a dealer in Passaic. He's very loosely connected to Joseph Russo, Jr.'s family, meaning he's an independent contractor who pays them a percentage so he can operate."

"And Marcus?"

"He came up with the same name," she says. "I don't know how; I guess just by being Marcus. Marcus is checking him out now."

"Knowing who he is and linking him to Gerald Kline's murder are two very different things," I point out.

"We can subpoena Lisa's emails and use that in court, right, Andy? The cops dropped the ball by not checking them in the first place."

Andy shakes his head. "Yes, we can use it, but it's possible the cops did check them. We don't know either way because we don't have access to discovery for Lisa's murder. But if Dylan wound up with it, he's in trouble for not turning it over because she mentions Kline might have been in danger from Rico as well. That's exculpatory evidence that he's obligated to disclose to us."

"The police didn't necessarily link the two killings," I say.

"They think Lisa could be a random drive-by and that she wasn't even necessarily the target. It's very unlikely they've checked an isolated email to an elderly woman in Somers Point from months ago."

"So what do we do with Rico?" Laurie asks.

"We pressure him," I answer. "Time for Simon to start pulling his weight around here."

RICO works out of a parking lot in downtown Passaic.

I don't know what his profit margin is like for his work selling drugs, but he's definitely not blowing his money on office space.

Marcus has been checking things out for the last two nights, and he has Rico's evenings down pat. From 8:00 P.M. until 10:00, he's out making collections from people who have obviously purchased their drugs on the layaway plan. It's possible that he's also handing off more merchandise to the buyers; it's been dark and Marcus hasn't been able to tell for sure without getting too close. That doesn't matter to us either way.

Once he is finished with these rounds, Rico heads back to an apartment building, where he presumably lives. He spends only about ten minutes there, so Marcus assumes he is picking up more merchandise for the rest of the night.

By ten thirty he is back in his spot at the parking lot; at that hour he has the place pretty much to himself. He clearly sees people by appointment since two purchasers are never there at once. He runs a fairly efficient operation.

Two men follow Rico around all night. They are obviously bodyguards, but they manage to stay out of the way, while clearly remaining ready to intervene if Rico has any problems.

Rico is about to have some problems.

Marcus and Laurie are going to neutralize the two body-guards and prevent Rico's customers from keeping their appointments. He seems to see people every fifteen minutes, so there shouldn't be that many customers to deter. The bigger issue will be the bodyguards, though Marcus specializes in big issues. In this case it's overkill; Laurie could probably handle it on her own.

Simon and I will have a chat with Rico. Andy and Laurie again said that I should not be a part of this, but I am not listening this time. It's my decision because it's my ass on the line. They disagree, but respect my right to make the call.

Simon is along because he majored in drug detection at the K-9 Academy, with a minor in scaring drug dealers. This job will be right up his alley.

We pull up in separate cars. Simon and I park one block east of the lot, and Marcus and Laurie park one block west. Laurie texts, "Ready?" I respond, "Let's do it." She must have seen the most recent customer leave, so we know the coast is relatively clear.

We get out of our respective cars and walk toward the entrance to the outdoor lot, which is where the two bodyguards are stationed. Simon and I get there first, when Laurie and Marcus are still about twenty feet away. "Hey, where you going?" one of the bodyguards asks.

"To talk to Rico." Then I point to the approaching Marcus.

"He said it was not a problem, that you guys would be cool with it."

Now they turn to Marcus and Laurie. "And who the hell are you?"

I think I see the second bodyguard reach for something in his pocket, but it is way too late. Marcus uses two punches to knock them both out cold, which I believe comes out to an average of one punch per bodyguard. I don't have time to check my math on that because I want to keep my appointment with Rico.

"Chuck, you good? What's going on?" Rico has obviously heard some commotion, probably the sound of his bodyguards hitting the cement.

He's in our sight line, so I say to Simon, "Hold." It is the command for Simon to keep the prey, in this case Rico, under control.

Even in the dim light, I can see the panic in Rico's eyes as a snarling Simon comes toward him. He starts to reach into his pocket, probably for a weapon, but I already have my gun trained on him and I yell, "Freeze, you piece of shit." I don't know Rico, but by definition I consider anyone who would attempt to shoot Simon to be a piece of shit.

Rico is smart enough to obey my command, as well as my next one, which is to slowly and carefully take the gun out and place it on the ground. The entire time he has his eye on Simon, who is now in pointing mode, meaning he has detected drugs.

What Rico doesn't know is that if I shoot him, I'll be digging my own legal grave. Killing people while out on bail is considered a major no-no in this jurisdiction.

"What's this about?" Rico says. "Whatever, we can work it out, you know?"

"Talk to me about Lisa Yates and Gerald Kline."

"Who are they?"

"They bought drugs from you, and you had them killed. I am

the guy you framed for Kline's murder after you had someone slit his throat."

"You got the wrong guy. Don't know them."

"You paid Jake Gardener to do it. We killed Gardener. You think we'll hesitate to kill you? Simon . . ."

Simon growls at Rico for effect. When Simon gets like this, even I'm scared of him, and he sleeps in my bed at night.

"Come on, I swear. I don't know any of these people. And any work needs to be done, I do it myself. I don't hire nobody."

"You're trying my patience, Rico. And you're pissing Simon off."

"You want money? You want merchandise?" Rico is starting to panic. "I'll give you whatever you want, but *I don't know those people.*"

I take out my cell phone and call Laurie, who answers on the first ring. "Call them in," I say.

"Okay."

We've planned it so that Laurie's friends in drug enforcement are waiting for her call. Within minutes they are on the scene, and after searching Rico and finding the drugs, they place him and his two friends under arrest.

I explain that we were walking Simon in the neighborhood, and he became aware of drugs in the area, from his time on the force in drug interdiction. The bodyguards tried to attack Laurie and Marcus, but they managed to fight them off. All of that constitutes the probable cause for the agents to have searched Rico, and what they come up with will put him on the sidelines for a long time.

It's a decent outcome, but not the one we wanted.

"I hate to say it, but I believed him."

We are back at Andy and Laurie's house to debrief about the evening.

"He would have said anything to save his ass; Simon had him scared to death. But he wouldn't cop to having killed Lisa and Kline because I don't think he knew what the hell I was talking about. And he didn't react to Jake Gardener's name at all."

"But we know for a fact that Lisa and Kline were buying from him, and that she was afraid of him," Laurie says.

I shake my head. "I wish that was true, but I don't believe it. You saw his operation; this is not a guy who was buying high-priced hit men. And Kline and Lisa were pretty well-off financially, especially Kline. He'd have a classier dealer; he wouldn't be going to that parking lot in Passaic with an envelope full of cash."

"There's always a chance we had the wrong Rico," Andy says. "Maybe among drug dealers Rico is like Smith, or Jones."

"Or maybe Rico is just the name the dealer used in dealing with Kline and Lisa," Laurie says. "Maybe his real name is Jeeves, or Shirley."

Andy is nodding. "Don't forget, Kline did a lot of traveling to do his seminars. He could have met Rico in any one of those places. But to cross-check all of those locations against places with drug dealers named Rico is not going to happen."

"Has anyone noticed that we seem to run into a lot of dead ends?" I ask. "We're chasing our tails here; no offense, Simon."

Andy nods. "But we still have the knowledge, and Lisa's email to back it up, that she and Kline were involved with drugs. That remains tremendously significant legally."

Sam calls to say that he has gone through Lisa Yates's phone records, but does not see any calls to Doris Landry or either of the two other people whose obituaries Lisa had. "I did find one other thing that might be of interest. Can I come over and show you?"

I ask that he come over this afternoon because I want to hear it and I have an appointment first. I'm going to see Richard Mahler, the guy who replaced Don Crystal as head of the IT department at Ardmore Medical Systems. Crystal said his name was "Miller, or Marler, or Marley, or some asshole," so even though he got the name wrong, he was damn close.

Mahler was reluctant to talk to me when I called him, so I used the Andy Carpenter technique of threatening him with a deposition. Threatening depositions tends to convince people to do things they would not ordinarily do.

Mahler, like his boss, Jason Musgrove, has an impressive office with the all-glass view of Route 17. I have to admit that it's hard to picture Mahler's predecessor, Don Crystal, in this office. I can't see him sitting behind this desk in his pajamas with feet, offering Tang to his corporate colleagues.

"Let's get this over with" is Mahler's congenial opening comment once I've sat down across from him.

"Works for me. You were Lisa Yates's boss?"

"For only a few months before she was tragically killed. I have only been with Ardmore for eleven months."

"Did you get to know her?"

"She did not report to me. I was only involved with her when there were computer-related issues, so I can't say I got to know her. The times we interacted she seemed pleasant and competent."

"Why did they hire you? What I mean is, why was there an opening?"

"If you met my predecessor, you wouldn't ask that question."

"Don Crystal? Wasn't he competent enough?"

"He was very competent, a terrific talent. His sanity, on the other hand, was open to debate."

"I've met him."

Mahler nods. "Then you know."

Point taken. Time to move on. "Was Lisa Yates involved in anything controversial? Anything that could have posed a danger to someone?"

"Not in her work life here at Ardmore. She had no discretion in what she did; data came in, she recorded it and put it into the system."

"Medical information?"

"Yes."

"Could she have added or deleted information that could have hurt someone?"

He shakes his head. "No. I assume you are looking for a motive for murder, but you won't find it here. If someone felt that Lisa was doing something like that, they could simply have filed a complaint, and an investigation would have restored the accuracy of the data. There would be no reason for physical violence. You need to understand, Lisa and others in her role are messengers, or really conduits, of information."

"Would you have seen what she was doing, on a day-to-day basis?"

"Only if I specifically looked at her work, but I would only have had reason to do so if there was a problem brought to my attention. I don't recall any issues coming up, so the answer to your question is no."

"Do you know why she quit?"

"Actually, I didn't realize she had quit until two weeks after the fact. I don't recall being surprised, but I didn't really expect it either. These things happen, especially recently. People with any level of computer skill are much in demand, so they move on to where they can make more money."

"Did you know Gerald Kline?"

"I knew of him, but we never met. When he recommended people, he went through HR, or Jason Musgrove."

"Were you aware of any involvement that either of them might have had with drugs?"

Mahler reacts with surprise. "No. Absolutely not. Where did that come from?"

I decline to tell him where that came from. I thank Mahler for his time and assure him that a deposition would have been more painful. I learned nothing, which seems par for the course.

"LIKE I said, Lisa Yates's phone records do not show calls to the people in the obits," Sam says. "Of course, they could have called her, and it wouldn't be in what I'm looking at. I basically have her phone bill information, which only shows outgoing calls. For the most part there is nothing unusual here, but one thing stood out. It could be nothing, but I thought you should see it."

"Good. Let's see it," Andy says.

"There's a woman named Jana Mitchell; she lives in Cincinnati. Lisa called her six times in the month before her death; I could check Mitchell's phone records, but I would guess she probably called Lisa as well."

"Why is this unusual?" I ask. "They could have just been friends."

"Well, for one thing, Lisa called her twice the day before she was killed, and the last call was just before midnight. That particular conversation lasted for forty-five minutes. I checked, and Jana

Mitchell works for Midwest Medical Networks. They do what Ardmore does, just in a different part of the country."

"So?"

"So it seemed strange to me that they talked so much on their personal phones, rather than their work phones. That, coupled with the timing, struck me as odd. But the other weird thing was that Lisa never emailed her. I checked through her emails twice . . . nothing there."

"That is interesting," Andy says. "Based on their jobs, these were computer people. They were close enough to talk all those times, but never email? Maybe they were afraid of security, of someone reading what they wrote."

"Right," Sam says. "Like I said, it could be nothing, but it struck me as strange."

I don't think any of us are tremendously confident that this is any kind of a breakthrough, but Laurie says, "Give me her number; I'll call her. Let's see what happens."

"She's probably at work now," I say.

"It's her cell number," Sam says. "Maybe she'll answer at work."

Sam gives Laurie the number and she dials it. Sam, Andy, and I can only hear Laurie's side of the conversation.

"Hello, is this Jana Mitchell?" There's a pause. "Hi, Jana, my name is Laurie Collins; I'm a private investigator in Paterson, New Jersey. I'm calling because I'd like to talk to you about Lisa Yates."

Another pause.

"You don't know her? I'm talking about the Lisa Yates who worked at Ardmore Medical Systems."

Another brief pause.

"Ms. Mitchell, is something wrong? We know that you and Lisa were . . ."

A final pause.

"Ms. Mitchell, I'm going to be out there tomorrow and I would really appreciate your talking to me. I think you know something that could be helpful to us in apprehending—"

Laurie hangs up the phone; Jana Mitchell apparently hung up on her first. Laurie turns to us. "I'm going to Cincinnati."

"What's going on?" I ask.

"Unless I am a terrible judge of people, Jana Mitchell was afraid, actually near panic. She was fine until I mentioned Lisa Yates, and then I could hear it in her voice. She also denied knowing Lisa, which is an obvious lie."

I totally trust Laurie's instinct in matters like this, but I'm frustrated that I can't go with her. Cincinnati is obviously outside the range that the terms of my bail allow me to travel.

"I'll go with you," Andy says.

She shakes her head. "You have to prepare for trial, and we also have a child, remember? A small person named Ricky? He has to eat. Hopefully he'll prepare meals for you as well."

"Ricky's a terrible cook," Andy says.

"So get pizza."

Andy brightens. "Now you're talking."

"Take Marcus with you," I say.

"Guys, are we now into protecting the helpless woman? I can handle myself, and I doubt that Jana Mitchell in Cincinnati is going to pose much of a danger."

I shake my head. "If she was really afraid, it means there is some danger involved."

Laurie ignores that and turns to Sam. "Can you get me her home address? I'll go see her after she's done with work."

"Duh," Sam says, meaning of course he can get her address. "I can also access her phone GPS and tell you where she is if she's not at home."

"Perfect," Laurie says. "I'll just book the flight and then it's off to Cincinnati."

"Go first-class," I say. "This defense team spares no expense."

LAURIE got a three o'clock flight out of LaGuardia.

It was a short flight, but she didn't need time to think about what her approach would be to Jana Mitchell. She had already decided that she would appeal to her on the basis of friendship. If Jana cared about Lisa Yates, then it was up to her to help find her killer.

There was always the possibility that Laurie was wrong, that Jana got scared simply because an investigator was asking her about a murder. The average person has no involvement in such things, and Jana could have just panicked, or at least flinched, in the moment.

But Laurie didn't think so. That Jana had denied even knowing Lisa was a tip-off. Laurie's instincts as a cop, and her instincts as a human being, told her differently. Jana's reaction was not normal. It was as if she had been fearing such a call, and her nightmare had come true.

Laurie didn't relish causing anyone a nightmare, and she was sorry she did something to trigger that fear. But it was part of her job, and that job was to help Corey. He wasn't going to prison for a crime he did not commit because Jana Mitchell was afraid. She would have to deal with it because Laurie was not going to let her off the hook—no matter what.

Laurie had some time to kill after landing and renting a car, so she grabbed a bite to eat. She did so in Clifton, the Cincinnati neighborhood where Jana Mitchell lived. There were nice restaurants and cafés there, and the weather was surprisingly cool and comfortable. She ate outside and it was extremely pleasant, and Laurie regretted not letting Andy join her. Then she realized that Andy would probably bemoan the lack of televisions showing sports, so she got over her regrets.

At eight thirty, she texted Sam Willis to ask where Jana's phone was.

"At her house," Sam said. "It's been there for almost three hours."

Jana's house was only eight blocks away, so Laurie decided to leave her car near the restaurant and walk there. That way she could quickly go over in her mind how she would approach Jana, and how she would deal with the woman's fear and probable unwillingness to cooperate.

When she was a block and a half away, she saw the flashing lights. As she got closer, her instincts once again kicked in, and somehow she knew that whatever was happening, it was at Jana Mitchell's house.

And it wasn't going to be good.

When Laurie got closer, police barricades kept the public away. Laurie did not know any of the Cincinnati cops, so all she could do was stand there with the neighbors and other onlookers.

Rumors were abounding, but one thing was certain: it was Jana Mitchell's house.

The prevailing view, at least among the neighbors, was that Jana was murdered. When Laurie saw the coroner's van, she had no doubt that it was true.

Laurie went to her hotel and turned on the local news. It was one of the lead stories. During a home invasion, a woman was killed in the robbery. They were not giving out a name, pending notification of next of kin, but reporters on the scene were talking with Jana Mitchell's house as a backdrop.

Laurie called Andy and told him what had happened. She asked him to call Corey and convey the news. She ended the call quickly; she did not feel like talking. She wanted to feel and deal with the full weight of what she had done.

This all started because Corey felt guilty about Lisa Yates; he felt that since he hadn't helped her enough the night of the domestic violence call, it led to her eventual murder. It had a certain logic to it, but Laurie had never felt his guilt was justified, even though he felt it sincerely. Nothing he could have done could have saved her all that time later.

But this situation was different. Anyone could draw a straight line from Laurie's call to Jana to her death. The fear Laurie detected was real, and it was proven to be thoroughly and horribly justified. Laurie was going to have to live with this for a long time.

Jana Mitchell was alive and well before Laurie entered her life. Twenty-four hours later she was the victim of a brutal murder.

But how did her killers find out about Laurie? Had Jana told them, whether intentionally or inadvertently? Why would she do that? On the surface it didn't make sense; if Jana was so guarded that she wouldn't talk to Laurie, why would she open up to someone else? Was it someone she trusted, but clearly should not have?

Had someone known that Laurie was traveling to Cincinnati to talk to Jana? How could they know that? Was Laurie being followed? Laurie doubted this theory; it seemed far more likely that the leak, if there was one, was from Jana's side.

The bottom line was that Jana must have known something crucial to solving the Lisa Yates murder, and crucial to helping Corey's case.

Whatever she knew died with her.

CARLOS called Musgrove on his way back to New Jersey.

He had flown to Cincinnati that morning; it was necessary to fly in so as to get his work done before the woman arrived. Obviously he had used a fake identification; he had plenty of those.

He was going to drive home, so as to make his steps harder to trace. It wasn't his idea; he considered it unnecessary and overly cautious. But he did as he was told. Those instructions included using a different fake ID when he rented a car and when he stopped for the night at a hotel, midway in the ten-hour drive that night.

"Everything went as planned, boss," Carlos said.

"I've seen the news coverage. I trust you made no mistakes?"

"No. I made it look like a home-invasion robbery, as we discussed."

"That may fool the police. It will not fool our adversaries."

Carlos waited for his boss to continue. He might hang up, or he might give Carlos further instructions. Carlos had reported in, so basically had nothing else to say. The boss was not much for chitchatting.

Musgrove was trying to deal with the implications of what he had just said to Carlos. The home invasion would not in fact fool the people that they were up against.

Carlos had made the original mistake of framing the ex-cop, Douglas, and they were still paying the price for it. Had Carlos not done that, Douglas and the others would have backed off by now. But because Douglas was facing murder charges, they would never back off.

Musgrove and his team had considered killing Douglas. If they did so, obviously his colleagues would no longer need to prove him innocent; the legal system would have no reason to go after a dead man.

There was always the chance that those colleagues, the lawyer and his coinvestigators, would continue the hunt, trying to avenge Douglas's death. But Musgrove felt they would likely do so with less energy and tenaciousness. If he was wrong about that, then they would pay the price as well.

Eliminating Douglas might well cause the police to reopen their investigation into Gerald Kline's murder, although they could take the easy way out and believe that the real killer, Douglas, was now dead. Either way, they had nothing to go on, and they would soon drop it and move on to other things.

Case closed.

It was a big decision, but Musgrove was ultimately a logical person, and the correct strategy was fairly clear. He would discuss it with his team, but knew that they would agree. They were even more ruthless than he was.

"Kill Douglas," he told Carlos. "But plan it carefully and do not fail."

"I know exactly how Laurie must feel," I say.

It's almost midnight and I'm still trying to come to grips with what happened in Cincinnati. Andy didn't have much information when he called beyond that Jana Mitchell had been murdered, and that Laurie would be heading home in the morning.

Dani was at a work event and got home at about eleven. I told her what happened, and we've been talking about it for almost an hour. Mostly I'm talking and she's listening.

"Telling her that she is not responsible won't help," I say. "It didn't help when they told me I wasn't responsible for Lisa Yates, and the truth is that there is much more of a cause and effect here. But where she is wrong will be in taking all the blame on herself. We were all a part of it; every step of the way. Laurie was the one who went out to Cincinnati, but if I was allowed, it would have been me. Either way we all agreed on the best approach."

"Obviously, it's a terrible tragedy," Dani says. "And just as obviously the best thing you can do now is catch the person that did this. Do you think the same person also killed Lisa Yates and Gerald Kline?"

I shake my head. "No, that was Jake Gardener. He admitted it the night he died. But that doesn't matter; the same people are behind it."

"This is not my area of expertise, but it seems to me that the big question at this point isn't who did it, it's why. Once you learn the why, the who will fall into place."

"You're exactly right. You sure you're not a cop?"

"Pretty sure. So what does what happened in Cincinnati tell you?"

"That whoever we are dealing with has a long reach. That it has nothing to do with a drug deal involving Rico or anyone else. We'll reach out to the Cincinnati cops and try and find a Rico out there, but we'll come up empty."

"But you know for a fact that Lisa was afraid of Rico, and that Kline was involved," Dani says.

"That's true, but that doesn't mean Rico caused her death. Lisa and Kline could have been involved in a lot of bad stuff. But what happened in Cincinnati also tells me that all of this is likely tied into Lisa Yates's work."

"Why?"

"Because that's the only consistent thread that runs through this. Lisa and Kline met through the medical services industry. She quit her job around the same time she was starting to worry; that's when she reserved the motel room. And Jana Mitchell was also involved in that industry."

"But you told me that Lisa was not a decision maker, all she did was input data into a computer and then make it available."

I nod. "That's what Richard Mahler and the guy he replaced, Don Crystal, both told me. They were above her, at least in the computer area, so they would know. Her coworker Susan Redick said the same thing as well."

"What does that tell you?"

"It's got to be something she uncovered. Maybe Kline was doing something illegal, but more likely not. He was not an employee of Ardmore; he had nothing to do with them on a daily basis. But she could have confided in Kline; they were lovers. That could be why he had to be eliminated as well."

"And Lisa confided the same thing to Jana Mitchell? Why?"

"I'm just guessing here," I say. "But they might just have been friends. They were in the same industry; maybe they attended conventions together. Maybe their paths crossed some other way at one point in their careers; for all I know they once worked at the same place. I don't know any of that yet; but I need to find out in a hurry."

"Does any of what has happened help you legally?"

"Not according to Andy. We can't connect any of it to the Kline murder, at least not well enough to get it in front of a jury. But I have seen Andy in court; he can be resourceful."

"Does he think you can win?"

"I haven't asked him yet. I'm afraid of the answer."

LAURIE has clearly been affected by the Jana Mitchell murder.

She acknowledges it at the beginning of our noon meeting. Andy and Sam are also here, but Marcus is not.

"I'm sure you know how I feel," Laurie says. "Andy obviously knows because I kept him up on the phone most of the night. Corey knows because he felt the same way about Lisa Yates." She smiles a sad smile. "Sam, you're off the hook."

She continues, "The only way I can deal with it is for us to catch the people that did it. So that's where my focus is."

I'm impressed by her, and not for the first time. She's a professional, and that's how she is handling it.

"Sam, can you check airline travel records?" I ask.

"Piece of cake. I can tell you who was on a flight, what class of service, and whether they ordered a kosher meal."

"Perfect. I want to know who flew from any of the New York

airports to Cincinnati yesterday and flew back either last night or first thing this morning."

"I'll be on that list," Laurie says.

"That's okay; I think we can eliminate you as a suspect. There's a good chance that whoever killed Jana Mitchell was sent from here; it seems unlikely that these people would have a Cincinnati hit man waiting in the wings for an assignment."

"I'm on it," Sam says. "Anything else?"

"Not now, but I'm sure there will be."

I turn to Andy. "What impact will all this have on our case?"

"Hard to say. If we can connect the deaths of Lisa Yates and Jana Mitchell to Gerald Kline, that would be helpful. That shouldn't be hard with Lisa because we have the email she sent to Doris Landry saying that she and Kline were worried about Rico. And we can show they had a relationship.

"But it would be especially helpful to connect Mitchell to Kline, since your GPS bracelet represents an ironclad alibi. Right now the difficulty will be in getting this in front of the jury; at this point we can't pass the threshold to get it admissible. I'm going to subpoena the phone records for both women; that will at least show that they had a relationship. But more of a connection would be helpful."

"Maybe I can help with that," I say. "It's a shot in the dark, but you never know."

I place a call to Stephanie Downes, Kline's partner, at least in name, in their business. I'm expecting to have to leave a message, but she answers the phone herself.

"Stephanie, this is Corey Douglas."

"Hey, Corey," she says, as if we're buddies and talk all the time.

"I didn't expect you to answer your phone."

"Why? Where did you think you were calling? Buckingham Palace? We're now a two-person firm and the other person went out for coffee. What's up?"

"I want to know if Gerald Kline was instrumental in hiring a woman named Jana Mitchell to work at Midwest Medical Networks in Cincinnati."

"I don't have a clue."

"Would you have records that would have a clue?"

"Possibly, but it will take some time. Did I mention we are a two-person firm?"

"I believe you did. The faster you could—"

"Why do you want to know?"

"Jana Mitchell was murdered last night."

"Whoa . . . let me put you on hold. I'll be back."

Her phone system has music playing when the caller is on hold, as most of the systems do. This system has two major positives: For one, it plays music by U2. For another, it doesn't keep interrupting to tell me how important my call is to them.

In this case, I listen to U2 for almost ten minutes; I think Stephanie must have forgotten me, deliberately or not. I'm about to hang up when she comes back on the line.

"Got it. Jana Mitchell attended a seminar at the Cincinnati Hilton two years ago. Gerald wound up interviewing her and recommending her to Midwest. They obviously hired her, though our records don't show that. So your apparent instinct is correct."

"Thank you, Stephanie. If I asked you for a list of all the people recommended that got hired by Ardmore and the other companies that do the same thing, could you get it for me?"

"I'm afraid not. Once Gerald or I would recommend someone, then it's up to the individual companies to decide one way or the other. They don't even necessarily communicate their decision to us, at least not formally. They might do it in a phone call, but I wouldn't have a record of that."

"Okay, I understand. Thanks, Stephanie; I appreciate the help."

"Anything I can do. Just call."

I get off the phone and tell Andy and Laurie what I've learned, that Jana Mitchell was recommended by Gerald Kline. "That means it has to be connected to the business," I say. "Something is going on in that world, some secret, that has gotten three people killed."

"I'm not saying you're wrong," Laurie says. "And I'm not saying we shouldn't pursue it; of course we should. But it's a conclusion we cannot take as fact. Yes, the three people were connected to that industry, but that is also how they met. Kline and Lisa were in a relationship; Jana and Lisa were friends. They could have been involved in something outside of their business world, something that they couldn't handle. Let's not forget Lisa's Rico email to Doris Landry; that is the one piece of tangible evidence we have."

"They were killed because of something they knew," Andy says. "That much seems clear. It's more likely than not that the secret is related to business, but I agree with Laurie that it isn't necessarily the case. The drug angle also remains a definite possibility."

Laurie frowns. "The problem is that the business end of it is basically impenetrable, at least to us. We have no idea what we're looking for, and no way to look. Sam could probably get into their systems, but the data would be enormous, and he'd be feeling around in the dark."

"I may have a way in," I say. "He could be our answer, even though he wears pajamas with feet."

THE digital clock on my night table says 2:31 A.M.

Simon is up and alert, emitting a low growl that tells me that he has detected something. Simon is not subtle when it comes to situations like this.

Waking up fully at this point is easy and instinctive for me; I've learned that when Simon is alert, I had damn well better be alert as well.

I get out of bed quickly and shake Dani awake, motioning for her to be quiet. "What?" is all she can muster; she doesn't understand Simon like I do.

"I believe there is someone in the house," I whisper. "Take the phone, go into the closet, and call nine-one-one. Talk softly, but tell them there is an intruder in the house . . . with a gun."

"There is?"

"Trust me; whoever is in this house didn't bring a bottle of wine as a housewarming gift."

"I want to help."

"You can help by calling the police. Now, Dani. There's no time."

"Be careful."

"Not to worry. We've got this."

She quickly gets up, grabs the phone, and goes into the closet, closing the door behind her. I've already taken my gun out of the night table drawer. Later I will stop and think about why I am approaching this moment with an anticipation that borders on relish, but this isn't the time.

I'm not going to leave the bedroom; I'm going to let the son of a bitch come to me. I put some pillows under the covers so it appears a person is there. It's a trick they do in the movies and on television; I just hope it works as well in real life. Even if it doesn't, Simon and I will take care of things.

We have the home field advantage.

Simon gets even more tense, so I know the enemy is approaching. "Stay," I whisper, so that he is about five feet to the right of the door. I am a little farther away on the left side. He obeys, as he has every time for the past eight years.

We're ready and waiting.

We don't have long to wait. I see his gun before I see him. He calmly and deliberately fires three bullets into the bed where Dani and I had been sleeping; there is no deafening sound because his gun has a silencer. He then steps into the bedroom to admire his handiwork.

Big mistake.

"I think you missed, asshole. Freeze and drop the gun."

He doesn't drop it, so I say, "Take him, Simon."

The intruder had been looking at me, so he is stunned when Simon leaps through the air and comes down with his teeth on the hand holding the gun. The guy screams in pain as the gun hits the floor.

"Off, Simon," I say, and he lets go of the arm. He takes a position three feet from the guy, still in pouncing position. He's having a great time; we both are.

"You just made a big mistake," the intruder says.

I've got to admire his guts; he seems completely unafraid. I'm holding a gun on him, and Simon is eyeing him like he's a Milk-Bone. "I made a mistake? You just pumped three bullets into a pillow. Now who sent you here?"

"Kiss my ass."

Suddenly, with a swift, almost imperceptible movement, a gun appears in his hand. It's small, almost pocket-size; it could have come out of a box of Cracker Jack, but it was probably hidden in his sleeve.

Simon sees it as I do, and he growls and starts to go for it. The intruder instinctively turns the gun toward Simon, so I shoot the man in the head. Despite that his actions had shown a lack of brains, I know he had one because it is now splattered back against the wall.

No one threatens Simon with a gun and gets away with it.

No one.

I go to the closet door and open it. "They're on the way," Dani says. "Is it over?"

"Yes, you can come out. But it's not a pretty scene. You might want to go downstairs."

She comes out and, instead of taking my advice, looks straight at the gunman. "Oh, my God."

"Please call Andy and tell him to come over right away. Laurie won't be able to come as well because of Ricky, so tell them it's important that Andy is the one to come."

"Okay."

"When the police arrive, send them up."

"You okay, Corey?" She's obviously concerned. "Is there anything else I can do?"

"I'm fine . . . never better. Just make sure Andy comes over right away."

THE police arrive three minutes after Dani goes downstairs.

I can hear her talking to them, though I can't make out what they are saying. They will not fully believe her, taking no chance that she is not the intruder herself. It's standard procedure; trust no one until all the players are fully identified.

I can hear them coming up the stairs. I quickly reach into the shooter's pocket and take his phone out, then put it into my own pocket. When the cops reach the room, I hold my hands up in the air. "I'm Corey Douglas and this is my house. I killed an intruder in self-defense. My gun is on the bed; his is still on the floor."

"I know who you are, Corey; you are having one shitty month."

I am much relieved to see that the cop just entering and doing the talking is Juan Ramirez, known to his fellow cops and friends as Johnny. Johnny and I go back a ways; he was one of my closer friends on the force.

"Johnny, you have no idea."

He looks at the guy on the floor. "One shot?"

"That's all it takes. But he fired three shots into the bed. I happened not to be in it at the time."

Johnny turns to Simon and smiles. "Simon, you witnessed the whole thing?" Johnny used to bring biscuits to work and slip them to Simon when he thought I wasn't looking.

"Simon was an active participant. Just like the old days."

"Robbery-Homicide will be here in a few," Johnny says. "You know the drill better than me."

"Can I go downstairs with Dani?"

"Sure."

So I go downstairs. Dani is sitting on the couch, her hands folded in her lap. She's got to be shaken up, but she's trying not to show it. This is not the kind of stuff she's used to.

"You okay?"

She nods. "A little shaky, but basically okay. Why was he here, other than to kill you?"

"I don't know yet; I don't even know who he is."

The door opens and Pete Stanton comes in with one of his lieutenants. It's another break for me; as the captain in charge of Homicide, he wouldn't as a rule take a late-night call. My guess is that he was told it was my house, so he made an exception. If that's the case, I appreciate it.

"Everybody having fun?" he asks.

"Barrel of laughs," I say.

Just then Andy walks in; it's getting crowded in here.

Pete sees him. "Well, look who's here."

"Did you botch the investigation yet?" Andy asks.

Pete goes upstairs to survey the scene. The coroner and forensic people arrive, so when Pete finally comes downstairs, he, Andy, and I go into the kitchen. Pete interviews me and

I tell him exactly what happened. I say that Dani will confirm it all. She'll be questioned after me, either by Pete or one of his people.

Pete tells me that I'll have to sign a statement attesting to everything I told him. Andy is silent throughout, meaning he finds nothing objectionable in Pete's questioning.

When that questioning is over, Andy asks Pete, "Did you identify the shooter?"

"According to his ID, his name is Carlos Evaldi. One of my people upstairs is familiar with him. He's a pro; a private contractor who works on his own for big money. Good that you were able to handle him, Corey."

"Simon made it happen. He's still the best cop I've ever been around."

It's another hour and a half before the house empties out. Andy is the last to leave, telling me that we'll talk in the morning. He looks at his watch. "Actually, it is morning."

"How is this going to play legally?"

He smiles. "It could definitely work in our favor."

"Maybe this will help as well." I take a phone out of my pocket and hand it to Andy. "It's the shooter's. Sam might be able to do something with it."

"You took it off him?" Andy asks, obviously surprised that I would do something like that, since it could be filed under *E*, for "evidence tampering."

"I did."

He smiles. "You might be my favorite client."

Andy leaves and it's just Dani, Simon, and me. "I'm going to make some coffee," she says. "No way I can go back to sleep."

"I can't either," I say, although the truth is that I could easily fall asleep. I am feeling completely calm.

Later we're sitting in the kitchen drinking coffee. I've given

Simon a chewie as a reward for his work tonight. Considering the quality of that work, he is way underpaid.

"I'm sorry about this, Dani. You shouldn't have to deal with crap like this."

"Has anything like this ever happened to you before?"

"You mean has someone broken into my house and tried to kill me? Or have I ever sent a woman into a closet to call nine-one-one? No, both those things are a first for me."

She studies my face. "You enjoyed it. On some level it invigorated you; it's like you clicked into gear."

I think about that for a few moments. "I'm afraid you're right. In situations like that, some instinct kicks in. It's who I was, and maybe it's who I still am. Actually, you can remove the *maybe* from that sentence; it's definitely who I still am."

"It was strange to see you in that moment. You weren't nervous at all; I was in a panic."

"It's all a question of what you're used to. I'd freak out if the caterer forgot the pot stickers."

She smiles. "I don't think you would."

"Me and Simon, we're both trained for this; we react in the moment. It helped us survive a lot of close calls over the years. I just wish you didn't have to go through it."

"You're a cop. You'll always be a cop." She doesn't make it sound judgmental; it's more just a statement of fact.

"I guess I am. Is that okay for you?"

"Everything about you is okay for me."

THERE is more publicity about last night's events than there was for the Kline killing.

I suspect Andy is behind that, and he gave an interview to the local paper, which is featured on the front page. Andy's friend Vince Sanders is the editor, so I'm sure Andy must have called in a favor. I'm also sure that Vince was happy to land the exclusive.

Andy previewed what our defense is going to be. People are getting killed all over the place, and in light of that it's ridiculous that I'm the one being charged. He said it more subtly than that, and he doesn't mention Jana Mitchell, but he cryptically refers to related murders that he will prove beyond any doubt that I could not have committed.

But the overall thrust of the interview is that the break-in at my house demonstrates conclusively that I am a potential victim, not the perpetrator. They tried to eliminate me because they feared I was getting close to finding out the truth. That's the Andy version, and it has the advantage of probably being the truth.

I have to put it behind me, and that's what I'm doing today. I called Don Crystal and asked for another meeting. He jumped at the opportunity when I told him I wanted his help in possibly bringing down Ardmore Medical Systems. It's not completely true, but close enough.

I asked if we could meet at a restaurant, and his response was "Are you buying? Because if you're buying, I'm eating."

"I'm buying. Anywhere you want that we can talk; if you pick a fancy place, you can wear your dress pajamas."

He chooses an Italian restaurant a few blocks from his house. I get there first, and when he walks in, I notice that his hair is actually brushed into some semblance of order. He wears shorts, tall white socks with sneakers, and a Led Zeppelin T-shirt.

We talk a little bit, but he's focused on the menu. It seems like he's been on an all-Tang diet for a while and is ready to come off it. He orders a full portion of pasta Bolognese as an appetizer, and chicken parmigiana as a main course. I order a salad and chicken paillard.

"So tell me how we're going to screw Ardmore," he says.

"That's not how I'd phrase it. I want you to tell me what could be going on there."

"What does that mean?"

"I'm going to be straight with you. Three people have been murdered. Gerald Kline, Lisa Yates, and Jana Mitchell."

"Don't know the last one. She worked at Ardmore too?"

"No. She worked at Midwest Medical in Cincinnati, and she was a friend of Lisa Yates."

"Okay. Got it. Keep going."

"I believe that it's all connected to something happening at

Ardmore, and maybe at Midwest. And for all I know, other companies that do the same thing as well."

"But you don't know what is happening."

I nod. "I don't know enough about the business to figure out what they could be doing. That's where you come in."

"How the hell would I know? I've spent the last year in my pajamas."

"But you designed the systems."

He frowns; I think he's disappointed at the realization that we are not about to bring Ardmore down. "They could have done whatever they want to them since."

"I think it's possible this has been going on for a long time; maybe even including while you were there."

"You think I did something crooked?"

"Did you?"

He laughs; if he's offended, he's hiding it well. "You think they left their systems open so the fired IT guy can walk right in and steal stuff? Or worse?"

"You ever see the movie *WarGames*? It was all about this computer that controlled whether we would go to war or not. Anyway, the guy who designed it had retired, but he still kept a backdoor password that let him back in after he was gone."

"Of course I saw it. It was all horseshit."

"Okay, so if you're not the bad guy, maybe that's why they got rid of you. Maybe they were afraid you'd figure it out."

He nods his approval; that's an explanation he can live with. "So what are they doing?"

"That's what I need you to tell me. You know the business— where is the money, and how could they be stealing it?"

He thinks about it for a while. "Maybe insurance?"

"What do you mean?"

"Well, if you're trying to get medical insurance, your ability to get it and the size of your premium would depend on your medical records. If the company could manipulate those records, you might look healthier to the insurance company than you really are."

"So how does Ardmore benefit from that?"

He shrugs. "Beats the hell out of me; cancel that idea. What about blackmail?"

"What about it?"

"This is personal information they are dealing with, you know? Maybe there are things that people don't want their employer, or their spouse, or whoever, to know. Maybe you're applying for a job as a minister and you want it kept secret that you've had thirty-eight cases of the clap. There's also mental health stuff in there. Maybe you don't want your future employer to know that you were arrested for dancing across the George Washington Bridge singing the score from *Hello, Dolly!* Or maybe you're a politician who doesn't want the voters to know that you get electric shock treatments every Tuesday and Thursday."

"You think that's really possible?"

"Those bastards would do anything. They could scour through the information, match something embarrassing up with someone they know has a lot of money, and there you go. And the suckers wouldn't even know that the bad guys were at Ardmore or Midwest; they'd have no way of knowing how they got the information."

"Would the CEO, Musgrove, have to know about it?"

"He wouldn't have to, but I'd bet he does. He's a slimeball."

"How could I confirm this?"

Crystal shrugs. "Maybe find some of the victims? That's your job, not mine. By the way, did you ask your former cop friends if they need a computer guy? I could be in charge of the union stuff. And if any bad things came up, like a cop took a payoff, I'd bury it in a cyber file where no one would find it."

"I'll talk to them. Sounds great."

"Bullshit; you're not going to talk to them. All you cops lie through your teeth. Just for that, I'm gonna have the tartuffo; it's unbelievable."

"THESE guys are really good," Sam says. "I ran into a dead end on the phone."

He's talking about the phone I lifted off Carlos, the guy whose brains I spent the morning wiping off my door and wall. If I have ever spent a more disgusting hour, I can't remember when.

Dani was at work and even Simon left the room; his attitude was that all he did was chew on the guy's arm. He had nothing whatsoever to do with the brain spatter; that's my problem.

"What does that mean?" I ask, although *dead end* is a pretty obvious visual. I just want a sense of what Sam considers really good.

"Well, Carlos made very few calls from that phone, only eleven in the last three months. They were all made to one particular number. Unfortunately, that number was just a routing device to another phone, or phones. So the phone he actually spoke to was hidden."

"No way to get to it?"

"No way. Like I said, these guys are good."

This conversation has not been a good way to start the day. It's about to get even worse; I've asked Andy to update me on where we stand heading into the trial.

Simon and I head over to Andy's. He and Laurie don't know it yet, but I'm going to ask them to take care of Simon if I wind up in prison. I can't think of better people to adopt him, especially since he's such good friends with Tara.

So far I haven't been able to bring myself to have the conversation; it's as if verbally recognizing the possibility makes it more likely to happen. But my head is not so far buried in the sand that I'm able to completely shut reality out. Over 90 percent of jury trials end in conviction on at least some of the charges; maybe I'll be the exception, but more likely not.

Andy and I go into his den; at the kitchen table Laurie and Ricky are playing some kind of board game that is bewildering to me. She keeps moaning and Ricky keeps laughing, so my guess is that he's winning. Laurie shows no inclination to join us in the den; maybe she doesn't want to face the bad news either.

"So where are we?" I ask, as soon as we're seated.

"I wouldn't say we're in deep shit. Probably waist-high. Dylan has two main things going for their side. One, you hated Kline and believed that he was a killer. You felt that you let Lisa Yates down by not arresting him the night of the domestic violence call, and you wanted to ease your guilt by nailing him."

"That's a little strong."

Andy nods. "It's their characterization, not mine. But you did basically say that out loud, and to a cop, no less. The second and more important piece of their case is the murder scene itself. You were there, obviously, and your bloody clothes were found not far from the scene."

"Both of those things are true."

Andy nods again. "Yes, they are, and they are going to have to be explained by us."

"Can we do that?"

"Maybe, maybe not. But whether the jury will buy it is another matter."

This is depressing, but no more so than what I expected. "So that's their case; what is ours?"

"We have to be able to point to the chaos going on around us. Lisa Yates, Jana Mitchell, and now Carlos Evaldi have all been killed, in addition to Kline. We have to show that there is some unseen killer out there operating in service of some unknown conspiracy. One problem is that *unseen* and *unknown* are not words that juries like. They want to make someone pay for the crime, in this case Kline's death. You are their only tangible choice right now."

"You said one problem. . . ."

Andy nods. "Right. The other problem is that we need to be able to get those other deaths in front of the jury in the first place. The judge has to find them relevant to the Kline case, otherwise he'll rule them inadmissible."

I already knew this, but it's still difficult to hear. "Any good news in this?"

"Absolutely," Andy says, surprising me. "Lisa Yates's death is the easiest for us to get in, since the prosecution will open the door by using Lisa as part of your motive. You were avenging her death."

"So it makes no sense that I would have killed her."

"Right. And if you didn't, then someone else did. Their counter to that, of course, would be to imply that Gerald Kline killed her. They'll say that you were right in thinking Kline did it, but that doesn't justify your slitting his throat. You positioned yourself as judge, jury, and executioner, which are three major no-no's.

"Jana Mitchell is the tough one. The Cincinnati police see it as a home invasion. We have an uphill fight to make our judge believe it is tied into our case."

"And Carlos?"

"Basically works for us. You are investigating to find the real bad guys, so they tried to silence you. That has the advantage of probably being true. But their position might be that Carlos was an associate of Kline and was avenging his murder. Or more likely that he had nothing to do with this case at all and was getting revenge over something you did in your days as a cop."

"Can we win?"

Andy pauses a moment. "We can win, but if you were betting it, you'd want odds. I could use some more bullets in the defense gun."

"That's what I wanted to talk to you about. I can't supply those bullets by sitting in court all day. I need to be out in the world, investigating."

"Don't go there. That's a nonstarter. You have got to be in court."

"Is that a rule?"

"It's my rule. Legally, you don't have to be there. It's your right to confront your accusers, but not your obligation. But your not being there would be a disaster."

"Why?"

"Two reasons. First of all, the jury will look negatively on it. They'll think that you don't give a shit about what's going on and what they're doing. It's arrogant. Secondly, it will negatively impact your ability to appeal certain issues if we lose."

"I'm trying to get us not to lose."

Andy shakes his head. "Laurie and Marcus will be working on it, and you can help them on nights and weekends. But when court is in session, you need to be there."

I'm not happy about it, but Andy is the expert and I promised to follow his advice. "Okay."

"Good. You have a nice suit to wear?"

"The last suit I wore was to my friend Bobby Rosenberg's bar mitzvah."

"Sounds perfect, but leave the yarmulke at home."

AMONG the many things that are bugging me, two stand out.

One is Steven Landry, son of the deceased Doris Landry. Both Andy and I independently believed he was lying to us at breakfast that day. It was about relatively innocuous stuff, like did he notify his mother's many email friends about her death. And it was strange that he wasn't at all curious about why we were asking our questions. But if he lied, and we think he did, then that sticks out in any criminal investigation.

People lie for a reason, sometimes important, sometimes not. Unfortunately for this theory, Sam had checked him out and found nothing to cause suspicion.

The other thing gnawing at me is Rico. Unlike the Steven Landry situation, we have factual evidence of Rico's existence. Lisa spoke about her fear of him to Doris Landry in that email. If she feared for her life at his hands, and then shortly thereafter she was murdered, that makes him an important piece in finding her killer.

I don't believe that the Rico we confronted in the parking lot that night had anything to do with either Lisa or Kline, which leaves us with a missing Rico.

But I also believe that whatever is going on is tied into Ardmore Medical Systems. Could it be that Rico, whoever the hell he is, is somehow involved with Ardmore?

I could call Jason Musgrove or Richard Mahler, the CEO and the head of IT, respectively, at Ardmore and ask them if the name Rico rings a bell, but I don't want to do that. I don't want to reveal my knowledge of Rico at all, and even though I don't necessarily suspect Musgrove or Mahler of anything, they could inadvertently mention something to someone else.

Instead I call my pajama-footed, Tang-drinking, tartuffo-eating pal, Don Crystal. "I've got another question," I say, after he answers the phone with "Yo."

"Any chance we could do it over a meal? I know a great barbecue place."

"Not this time; you've got a rain check."

His sigh is audible. "Okay, what's the question?"

"Does the name Rico mean anything to you?"

"Like Puerto Rico?"

"No, like a person's name. I'm trying to find out if there's a person named Rico at Ardmore."

"Not that I can think of, but I still have a copy of the company phone directory somewhere. I could find it and look."

"I'd really appreciate that. One more question . . ."

"For a total of two? I should be sucking down a slab of ribs for this."

I ignore that. "Was there a drug culture at Ardmore?"

"A drug culture?" Whatever he thought I was going to ask, this clearly wasn't it.

"Yes. Were drugs prevalent there?"

"If they were, I'd still be there."

I laugh at that. "Thanks, Don . . . that was really helpful. Will you check the phone directory?"

"You got it. Next time, barbecue."

Having made no noticeable progress on the Rico front, I turn to our suspected liar, Steven Landry. He had little information to offer about Lisa Yates, other than that his mother liked her and tried to help her in the same way that she tried to help everyone else. There is a chance that Doris Landry was more open with her friends about it than with her son, who did not live near her.

I call him and say, "Steven, I had breakfast with you and Andy Carpenter the other day."

"Right."

"I wonder if you could help me with something. Can you give me contact information for some close friends of your mother? Maybe she shared information about Lisa Yates with them."

He hesitates, as if unsure how to respond. Then, "No way. I know who you are; you killed that guy."

"Actually, I didn't. But this is for Andy."

"I don't care who it's for. Leave my mother's friends alone."

Click.

ANDY warned me that jury selection would be total torture, and he was right.

The worst part, he cautioned me, was that while you make picks, you have no idea until the end of the trial if you chose correctly. He compared it to betting on a basketball game, but forgetting who you bet on. So you watch the game, and as each basket is scored, you have no idea whether it is good news or bad news.

That would be more than enough to stop me from watching the game, but I am forced to sit here and watch the jury selection. The thing that Andy did not tell me, but that I started realizing ten minutes in, is that it is also crushingly boring.

He says that he doesn't use jury consultants because he doesn't trust them any more than his own gut, even though he has no confidence in his own gut at all.

One of my problems is that I hate every single potential juror that is called up to the stand to answer questions. For one thing, I keep thinking, *Who the hell are you to judge me?* And then I picture each of them voting to send me to prison for the rest of my life, after which they go home to tell stories at parties about the cool time they had on jury duty.

I find myself wanting to strangle them with my bare hands, but that would mean another arrest for murder, another trial, and another awful session of jury selection to sit through.

That I cannot be out in the world, working the investigation and trying to prove my innocence, seems likely to cause my head to explode. Andy can tell what I'm going through, and a few minutes ago he leaned over and whispered a question: "Having fun?"

At the defense table with Andy and me is Eddie Dowd. Eddie played for the football Giants for a couple of years, then went to law school and is Andy's second-in-command when he has a case. Andy says that Eddie is an excellent lawyer and better than Andy when it comes to writing briefs and motions.

Dani is not here; I told her not to come. She reluctantly agreed, but insisted that she'll be here for the actual trial and has already notified her company that she's going to be taking her vacation days soon.

What I need to do is pretend to be interested in the voir dire, while instead thinking about the case and what I can do when I get out of here. I've brought a lot of documents with me, which I can go over during breaks. But I've committed so much of it to memory that I almost don't need to look at them.

During the first break, which will last a whopping ten minutes, I check my cell phone. There is a message from Dani asking me how it's going, and another from Don Crystal. He says that he's checked the Ardmore office phone directory that he has, and an Enrique Lopez is listed. Maybe his nickname is Rico?

Lopez is listed as working in the client management department, which means he keeps Ardmore's clients happy with their service. Crystal says he called one of his few remaining friends at Ardmore, who says that Lopez left the company two months ago, though the person did not know why.

"Might be worth checking out," Crystal says in his message. "If it comes to anything, you owe me a slab of ribs. If it doesn't, you still owe me a slab of ribs."

If it turned out to be meaningful, I would buy Crystal a herd of cows. But even though I doubt that it will go anywhere, I call Laurie and give her the information to check out. She says that she will get on it and asks me how it's going in court. "Jury selection can get boring," she says.

"I noticed."

When court resumes, I use the opportunity to reflect on my last meeting with Don Crystal. He offered two possibilities when I pressed him on what could be going on at Ardmore. One possibility was blackmail, that people at Ardmore were using sensitive and possibly embarrassing information on wealthy people as a threat to get them to pay.

It seems unlikely to me; whatever is being done is happening on a large scale. To pull off such a huge operation, it would require the blackmailing of a large group of people. At least some potential victims would balk and go public with what was going on.

The other possibility that Crystal mentioned seems even more unlikely. He said that someone at Ardmore could be adjusting the records to help people get insurance at a lower rate. If insurance companies see a potential client as a significant health risk, the premium would be higher.

I just don't see how the change in premiums could in any way pay off in the way the people running the conspiracy would need. They could charge people for adjusting the records, but the potential savings for those people would not be enormous. To pay the Ardmore conspirators a mere percentage of those savings is not nearly big enough to justify these murders.

I've been thinking that life insurance might be more interesting, if only because more money would be at stake. Life insurance policies can run to a million dollars, and sometimes more. A person's health history can be crucial in determining the premium one would pay, and even in getting insurance at all.

Where it falls apart, at least in my mind, is the Ardmore connection. How would they profit from it? As in the case of the medical insurance, clients paying a fee for Ardmore to adjust their medical records just wouldn't pay off on the kind of scale necessary to take these kind of risks, and to commit these kind of murders.

The only way it would make sense is if the bad guys could somehow get a large piece of the life insurance payoffs. But that again crumbles under any kind of analysis. Why would a beneficiary, a family member, turn over their money to someone at Ardmore?

Could Ardmore take out a secret policy, naming one of their own as a beneficiary? I suppose it's possible, but they'd have to know who was going to die relatively quickly, otherwise they would be paying the premiums for many years.

Might their knowledge of the person's health records help them predict who would die relatively soon? I suppose it's possible, but way too complicated and way too speculative.

Could they be taking out a policy and then murdering people? Is that what happened with the three people whose obituaries Lisa Yates was hiding? It just does not seem possible to be doing that on a large scale, and I'm not aware of any media stories speculating that any of those three people were murdered.

Since I know that Steven Landry is Doris Landry's only immediate surviving family member, I make a note to ask Sam to find out if he received a payout on any life insurance policy that she had.

Even if that is the case, I still don't know how that could benefit anyone at Ardmore. But it can't hurt to find out.

I also make a note to myself to check out the death certificates that Sam got for the three people. I want to see if there is even a hint that any of them could have been murdered.

This is what is known as grasping for straws . . . but it sure beats jury selection.

LAURIE was able to track down Enrique Lopez.

She initially called Jason Musgrove, who coldly told her that he was finished talking to anyone involved in my defense. Maybe the publicity about the upcoming trial has hardened his attitude, or maybe it is something else. I can't say either way, but if something is going on at Ardmore, as CEO, Musgrove would be in prime position to be involved.

Instead Laurie turned to Sam, who found Lopez's home address in Garfield. She went to see him, but came away close to positive that he is not our "Rico." He is in his sixties and retired due to failing health. She cannot see him as a dangerous drug dealer, and nothing he said to her changed that feeling.

Andy thinks that jury selection will be finished today, possibly by late morning. So far we have seated eight people, so we need four more and two alternates. I'll be delighted when we're done, although that means the trial will start. I am dreading the trial because I am more than a little worried about the outcome.

It takes longer than Andy predicted, and it's almost three o'clock in the afternoon before the fourteenth person is chosen. Judge Wallace gives them what amounts to a brief pep talk, thanking them in advance for their service and impressing on them the incredible importance of their task.

Dylan is pretty much beaming; he either thinks they got a pro-prosecution jury, or he's doing a good job of faking it. Andy, true to his preselection prediction, says he doesn't have the slightest idea whether we did well.

Judge Wallace says that we will begin opening arguments to-morrow. He admonishes the jury to be on time, and also not to watch any media coverage having to do with this trial, effective immediately.

We all head back to Andy's to go over last-minute pretrial preparation. Laurie told me that Andy has never before included his clients in these kind of things. She views it as a sign that he respects me; I think it has more to do with his clients usually being in custody during the trial.

Sam is here to report that Steven Landry did collect on an insurance policy on his mother's life, $525,000. The policy that was taken out three years ago. He placed the money into his invest-ment account and it is still there. He did not, obviously, give a portion of it to anyone at Ardmore or anywhere else for services rendered.

Andy's pretrial preparation session with me consists of his telling me to go home and get some sleep.

"Do you want to practice your opening statement? Laurie and I could listen and . . ."

I stop talking when I see Laurie cringing.

"I never prepare an opening statement," Andy says. "I wing it."

"You wing it?" I don't say so, but the concept horrifies me.

"Yes, I wing it. If it makes you feel better, I have a general idea of what I am going to say. If I were to practice it, I would lose the spontaneity."

"Do you ever forget anything?"

"I'm sure I must, but by definition I never remember what I forget." At this point Laurie is smiling.

"I'm going to get some sleep," I say.

"Good idea."

When I get home, I quickly realize that there is no chance I can get any sleep. Luckily Dani is here; since all this started, she has basically been here full-time. We hadn't talked about it; it just came naturally.

She knows I can use the support, but she does it in an unobtrusive way. She is here when I want to talk or vent, but gives me space when I need it, which is often. Tonight she makes some coffee and reads a book while I immerse myself in all these trial documents.

I am going over the death certificates for the three people whose obituaries Lisa Yates had in her suitcase. As Sam had said, nothing indicates any possibility of murder. Samuel Devers died of heart failure, Eric Seaver succumbed to complications from lupus, and Doris Landry died of pancreatic cancer.

Doris Landry's death certificate is the last one I look at. It was prepared by the coroner of Atlantic County, New Jersey, and lists Landry's name, gender, address, date of birth, date of death, and cause of death. It's standard stuff, but one thing about it strikes me as odd. I know I must be wrong, but I check it anyway.

The certificate was prepared on June 17 and lists the date of her death as June 16. I google New Jersey procedures and find that this makes sense: you can get a death certificate on a one-day turnaround.

But that is not what is strange. I look at the copy of the newspaper obituary that Lisa had in her suitcase. The date at the top of the page says June 15.

If the death certificate is correct, and death certificates usually are correct, then Doris Landry's obituary came out the day before she died.

"COREY Douglas was a police officer in Paterson for twenty-five years," says Dylan Campbell.

"By all accounts he served the community well, and I have no interest in disputing that. I'm sure he made mistakes, but we all do. But, ladies and gentlemen, you are not here to render judgment on Mr. Douglas's service as an officer, good or bad."

Dylan stands at the lectern as he talks. His style is formal, almost professorial. But he has a strong voice and he commands the room.

"You are here to decide whether or not Mr. Douglas brutally murdered one Gerald Kline, by slitting his throat with a knife and watching him bleed to death. It will not be a tough decision; we will place him at the scene along with his bloody clothing, and his bloody knife, all of which he unsuccessfully tried to hide. You will hear this evidence, and I believe that you will come to the conclusion that we have proven our case beyond a reasonable doubt.

"I brought up Mr. Douglas's police record for two reasons. One is to acknowledge his service, but the other, more important reason, is because during that service he made a decision that he came to regret.

"It haunted him ever since and caused him to hate Mr. Kline and to vow revenge. He swore a vendetta against Mr. Kline and he acted on it. He got his revenge in the most heinous way imaginable.

"Service as an officer does not allow someone to do what was done to Mr. Kline. You may not think that Mr. Kline was a good person, although many think that he was. And you may even think that Mr. Douglas was correct in despising him. But you cannot think that Mr. Douglas acted properly in committing this act; our society simply cannot function if such an act is not punished.

"You will see photographs that I wish you did not have to see. But you are here to do a job, perhaps the most important job any citizen can ever do. So you must not look away; you must tackle this head-on and face it down.

"I know you will. Thank you."

Dylan was effective; the jury seemed to hang on every word. Judge Wallace calls on Andy to give our side of it, and he gets up, ready to wing it.

"Ladies and gentlemen, Mr. Campbell and I agree on something, and it is likely to be the only thing we will agree on for the duration of this trial. And that is that Corey Douglas was a hell of a cop.

"Twenty-five years . . . and no matter who Mr. Campbell calls to the stand, you will not hear one negative thing about Corey's record in all that time. But you'll hear about his commendations, and his heroism . . . I'll make sure of that. His service is something to be proud of, and something we should all be grateful for.

"But it is true that everyone makes mistakes, and Corey Douglas believed he made one. He thought he should have gone overboard to protect a citizen that he thought was in danger. You will hear all about it, but understand one thing. He did not make a mistake; he acted properly and according to correct police procedure.

"But it bothered him; it bothered him a lot. That's because he was a good cop, and he cared about the people he had sworn to protect. He came to believe that Gerald Kline was a criminal, perhaps a murderer, and he set out to prove it. That's right . . . to prove it. He is now a respected private investigator, but he took on an assignment without pay, simply because he felt that he owed it to the person that he was unable to protect. It was not a vendetta, as Mr. Campbell would have you believe. It was a man doing his job, even though it was no longer his job.

"Do you know how Mr. Campbell became aware of this . . . of Corey's belief that Mr. Kline was likely a criminal who should be brought to justice? Because he made no effort to hide his presence at the scene; he was open about it. And that is because he fully intended to do things by the book, according to the law. And he also made no effort to hide his belief that Mr. Kline was a murderer, because he had no intention of taking the law into his own hands.

"But there is something else you should know, and it concerns a vast conspiracy that to this date has left three people dead, one of whom was Mr. Kline. You will hear about it and you will wonder who is behind this conspiracy, and what they are trying to accomplish.

"But you will know one thing: it is way bigger than Mr. Kline, and Corey Douglas, and you will wonder why Mr. Douglas is the person you have been called upon to judge.

"Thank you very much."

Andy comes back to the defense table and sits down. I lean over and say, "You are really good at winging it."

He nods and whispers back, "It's a gift."

"We need to talk after court. I found out something last night that is interesting and strange." Andy got to court a bit late this morning, and I didn't have time to tell him about the death certificate date conflicting with the obituary date.

"Okay. Let's meet at the house after court ends for the day."

Dylan's first witness is Sergeant Bill Glover, who was among the first cops on the scene at Kline's house the night he was killed. Dylan gets Glover to confirm that, as well as that a 911 call brought him there.

"Do you know who made that call, Sergeant?"

"Yes, it was Mr. Douglas."

"When you arrived, was Mr. Douglas the only person on the scene?"

"Well, Mr. Kline was there, but he was deceased. And Mr. Douglas's dog was there."

"That's a former police dog?"

"I believe so," Glover says.

"Did you question Mr. Douglas when you arrived?"

"I did not. Lieutenant Lillard from Robbery-Homicide was going to be there very shortly, so I was leaving that to him. My partners and I just made sure that there was no one else in the house, and that the area was secure."

Dylan continues questioning Glover, and even though he has nothing particularly interesting to say, Dylan uses up almost an hour to get him to say it.

Andy does not do much to challenge him, probably because he didn't do us any damage. He was just setting the scene, and everything he said was true. If Andy has any bullets in the defense gun, I assume he is saving them for more important witnesses.

Judge Wallace adjourns court until tomorrow, and Andy says, "I'll see you at the house."

I turn and see Dani sitting in the gallery as it starts to empty out. I hadn't realized she was here. "Okay. Dani and I will pick up Simon and meet you there. With me in court he's not getting out much."

"I'll tell Tara her boyfriend is coming over."

"And I'll call Sam; we're going to need him."

Andy smiles. "You're relying on Sam quite a bit these days." He's gently mocking me about my turnaround from my previous resistance to Sam doing his "extralegal" computer work.

"I know; I can't help it. It's like having an investigative genie."

"IT'S probably just a mistake," Laurie says. "Some bureaucrat put the wrong date on the death certificate."

"I'm not disagreeing," I say. "But there's been something about Doris Landry's death that's unusual. First, her son, Steven, lied to us at breakfast that day. Then he turns around and refuses to help when we asked him to connect us to his mother's friends. And now this. I'm not saying these are earthshaking events, but they're worth pursuing."

"What's your theory?" Andy asks. "That she was murdered?"

"No. I don't think so. Sam, can you find out if anyone other than Steven Landry was the beneficiary of a policy on Doris Landry's life?"

"Nope."

It's so unusual for Sam to say he can't do something that I do a double take. "Why not?"

"So much for your genie," Andy says.

Sam explains, "There's no place for me to look. I can't access the financial records of whoever that beneficiary might be because we don't know who it is. And there are way too many insurance companies; I'd have to know which company we're talking about."

"If you don't believe Doris Landry was murdered, then what is your theory?" Laurie asks.

"I'm not sure I'd call it a theory; that might be giving it too much credit. Let's say it's the germ of an idea."

"Fine. So what's your germ?"

"Insurance companies work on actuarial tables; they are essentially making bets based on percentages. So let's say that Ardmore supplies them with tampered patient information that indicates relatively good health, when the reverse is actually true.

"So the company writes the policy, and then when the patient dies much earlier than would have been expected, they have to pay off. In the meantime, whoever faked the data in the first place had taken out a policy and collects. They would not have to do this in too many cases to make many millions of dollars."

"How does this fit in with the different dates on the obit and the death certificate?" Laurie asks.

"It doesn't; I'm on to a new germ." I turn to Andy. "What do you think?"

"I think you're probably nuts, but it's worth pursuing. We have to get a look at Doris Landry's health records."

"Sam?" I ask.

He nods. "I'll give it a shot."

"Do that, but it's not enough," Andy says. "Even if we get them and it shows what we want, the information would have been obtained illegally and we couldn't use it in court. We'd have to then try and get it through legal means. By the time we did that, you'd be making license plates in Rahway."

"So what do we do?"

"I'll ask Jason Musgrove for it."

I shake my head. "He won't give it to you. If I'm right about this, and I admit it's a big if, he's got to be in on it. And Richard Mahler is as well. That's why they dumped Don Crystal; they didn't want him around when they made their move."

Andy nods. "I'm sure Musgrove won't go along with it; he'll cite privacy concerns whether he's dirty or not. In the meantime, I'll be trying to get Judge Wallace to issue a subpoena."

"Do you think he will?"

"Fifty-fifty."

Andy calls Eddie Dowd, explains the situation, and asks him to prepare a motion to subpoena the records. Andy wants to file it first thing in the morning.

When he gets off the phone, he says, "I've changed my mind. I'm not going to ask Musgrove for it."

"Why not?"

"He won't give it to me, especially if you're right and he's dirty. And if he learns that we want it, he could have it changed before we get the subpoena. If they can doctor the records once, they could do it again. This way at least Sam will have time to access the real data."

"I'm on it," Sam says.

"LIEUTENANT Battersby, why did Mr. Douglas ask to meet with you?" Dylan asks.

"He wanted to know if we were making progress on the Lisa Yates murder case."

Dylan gets him to explain that case for the jury, in case they are not familiar with it. Then he asks, "What was Mr. Douglas's interest in Ms. Yates's case?"

Battersby painstakingly tells the story that I told him that day, about my domestic violence call, my belief that Kline was guilty of hitting her, and my frustration that I couldn't do anything about it.

"Mr. Douglas expressed to you that he was holding a grudge against Mr. Kline?"

Battersby nodded. "I don't remember all of his exact words, but that was the general thrust of it."

"Do you remember any of his exact words?"

Battersby frowns; he doesn't want to be doing this. "Yes. He said he wanted to 'strangle' Kline."

Dylan turns the witness over to Andy, who asks, "When Mr. Douglas made the comment about strangling Mr. Kline, did you place him under arrest for threatening a citizen with death?"

"No, I—"

"Did you warn Mr. Douglas not to do such a thing?"

"No."

"Did you find Mr. Kline and warn him that an ex-cop was intent on killing him?"

"No."

"What did you do?"

"Well . . . I laughed."

"So you didn't take his comment seriously?"

"I did not."

"Okay, then when Mr. Douglas expressed an obvious interest in the Lisa Yates murder, wanting to know how your investigation was going, did you put him on your list of suspects?"

"No."

"Why not?"

"He was looking to find her killer. Why would he do that if he was her killer? Coming forward like that would have made no sense."

"Thank you. No further questions."

On redirect, Dylan asks, "Lieutenant, if at the time of that meeting you knew that at some time in the future Mr. Douglas would be in a house alone with Mr. Kline's dead body, would you have taken his threat more seriously?"

"I might have," Battersby says. "I suppose so."

Dylan next calls Tony Sciutto, a cop I served with in the Paterson PD. He worked in the records department, so I filed the domestic violence report with him. He's another obviously reluctant witness, but relates how I expressed my dislike for Kline and my frustration with not being able to arrest him.

Andy has little to ask him on cross; my dislike for Kline has already been established. All Andy does is get Tony to say that he did not view my attitude as a threat to Kline, and that Tony always knew me to be an outstanding cop.

Judge Wallace sends the jury home early so he can discuss our motion to subpoena Doris Landry's health records. Dylan, obviously, is opposed. "The defense has not even come close, they have not even made an effort, to show that whatever happened to Ms. Landry is relevant to this case."

Andy responds, "Your Honor, we will do more than make an effort, we will demonstrate relevance quite conclusively. But we will do it during our defense case, which is the appropriate time. It is not necessary for us to do so now because relevance is not a factor here.

"Federal law is quite clear; the deceased do not have a right to privacy in medical matters. This material is absolutely available under the Freedom of Information Act; we are asking for a subpoena because applying under that act would take far too long.

"There is some deference to state law in matters of this kind, but there is nothing in New Jersey law that contradicts it. We are entitled to this information by any standard, and a showing of relevance at this time is therefore not required."

Dylan says, "Your Honor, rather than take the defense's word for this, we would request some time to analyze applicable New Jersey law. As Your Honor knows, this was just sprung upon us."

Andy shakes his head, as if saddened. "I would have hoped that the prosecution team, as lawyers representing the State of New Jersey, would have been familiar with New Jersey law. The defense should not be delayed in the search for truth because the prosecution is uninformed."

Dylan looks like his head is about to explode. "That is outrageous, Your Honor."

"Which part?" Andy asks. "You just admitted you were uninformed. I was supporting your position."

"Gentlemen, do I really need to hear this childish bickering?" the judge asks.

Dylan and Andy both apologize, after which Judge Wallace says that he will authorize the subpoena. I'm relieved when Andy doesn't stick his tongue out at Dylan in triumph. Instead he asks the judge to insist on compliance with the subpoena immediately.

"All it takes is to go into the computer and print out the records," Andy says. "That should take a matter of minutes."

Wallace agrees and adjourns court for the day. Eddie Dowd will follow up and make sure the subpoena is served immediately.

"Nice job," I say, but Andy frowns.

"A temporary victory. Ardmore will now get involved and will appeal the decision. This could take forever; all we did was start the process."

That is bad news, obviously, and we're greeted with another piece of bad news when Sam calls me on the way home. "I can't believe I'm saying this, but I can't get into the Ardmore records."

"Why?"

"It's got at least two layers of encryption that are impenetrable without knowledge of the code. If our atomic secrets had this much protection, Ethel and Julius Rosenberg would be playing shuffleboard tournaments in a senior home in Florida."

"I was wrong," Andy says when I answer the phone.

"Is it good news or bad news that you were wrong?" I ask, not knowing what he was wrong about. It could be that he was wrong when he said we had a chance to win the case.

"Remains to be seen. They're not contesting the subpoena; we'll have the data by noon today. They're having one of their computer techs access it from home."

"I don't like it. If it was something helpful to us, they would be fighting it tooth and nail."

"That was my first reaction. Also my second and third. Why don't you come over at two; Eddie Dowd will be bringing it here. I'll have Sam here as well."

With time to kill, Dani, Simon, and I head out to an outdoor brunch. We don't talk about the trial or case at all, or how next week at this time I could be sitting in a cell. But even with that hanging over our heads, it's a pleasant respite and Simon seems to have a great time being doted on by two people.

The brunch ends early when it starts to rain. "Maybe this is an omen," I say.

Dani frowns. "Or maybe it's just rain."

I arrive at Andy and Laurie's just before two with low expectations, and they are met. Eddie Dowd had gotten here a little early, and they've gone over copies of Doris Landry's medical information.

Nothing is obviously out of order; Landry had a series of medical issues throughout her life. Back surgery, a torn Achilles, various infections . . . nothing that one wouldn't expect from someone who had already lived more than seventy years.

According to the records, her pancreatic cancer was diagnosed less than six months before her death. If that is true, then there would have been no issue in disclosure to insurance companies on a policy that was taken out well before that.

"That's that," I say. "So much for my germ of an idea."

Andy shakes his head. "Not necessarily. If we think they've manipulated the data once, then maybe they've done it here. Sam, Hackensack Hospital is the one who provided the information on the cancer diagnosis. Can you get into their system and find out if what they provided matches what is here?"

"I don't see why not," Sam says. "Give me a couple of hours."

He leaves, and thus begins the longest two hours of my life, or at least the longest since the other day during jury selection. The phone finally rings, and when Andy sees on caller ID that it's Sam, he says, "You take it."

I answer and Sam's news is quick and painful. "The hospital information matches what we got from Ardmore. It's legit."

IT'S rained on and off most of the night and into this morning.

An outdoor brunch is therefore out of the question, and an indoor one eliminates Simon's attendance, so that is equally unacceptable. So, Dani makes French toast for breakfast. It's not her specialty; actually, Dani doesn't have many cooking specialties. I haven't told her that, but I suspect she knows it because she's eating her efforts as well.

I'm still aggravated that yesterday proved to be such a nonevent, but that hasn't stopped me from thinking that the source of all that has happened is somewhere at Ardmore. Somehow, according to the already disproven theory that I can't let go of, they are screwing around with the data.

My current suspect in all of this is Richard Mahler, the head of IT, who replaced Don Crystal. Mahler obviously has the expertise and access to have done it, and that this all began when he was brought in is too much of a coincidence. I also think Jason Musgrove might be engineering the entire enterprise, but I'm nowhere close to proving that either of them is culpable.

I decide I should speak to Stephanie Downes about this, partially because she has the information I am looking for, and partially because she seems to be the only one willing to talk to me. I have no way of reaching her on Sunday because I only have her office number. I check the company website to see if I can email her; maybe she checks her emails on weekends.

I catch a break when I see that she is doing another seminar today at noon; this one is at the Saddle Brook Marriott, just ten minutes from my house. I don't know how long the seminars last, but I certainly don't want to sit through the entire thing. I'm guessing that it can't be less than an hour, so I arrive there at one o'clock.

The setup seems to be the same as last time, although Carol Ayers is the only woman at the desk outside the meeting room. It's possible her colleague left already, since obviously the crowd has long ago gone inside and gotten settled.

"Hello, Mr. Douglas," she says.

"Seventy-five bucks to have you take my picture?"

She smiles. "No charge and no picture this time; you missed most of the event."

I start to go in, but then stop. "What did you do when Gerald Kline and Stephanie held events in different places at the same time? How did you choose which one to work at?"

"They never did that; they would alternate." Carol smiles. "They probably didn't want to pay another employee."

I go inside, and sure enough, about fifteen minutes later Stephanie Downes finishes her spiel to substantial applause. Unfortunately, that is not the end of it. The attendees surround her afterward, trying to get her attention and make an impression. She stays gracious throughout and occasionally takes notes about what they say. She gives them all her card.

When it's all over, she walks over to me. "Sorry that took so long."

"No reason to apologize. You're a medical services rock star."

She laughs. "Not hardly. They want me to recommend them for a job. That's why they're here." Then, "But I'm guessing that's not why you're here. You're here for more information."

"That's uncanny."

Another laugh from her. "So what is it this time?"

"There's another person that I want to know if Gerald Kline recommended for his job."

"As I told you, I wouldn't necessarily have that information, but I might. Either way I won't be able to access it until tomorrow when we get in the office."

"I understand."

"Who is it?"

"Richard Mahler."

"Oh, that one is easy. I didn't get involved because I've known him forever; we literally went to high school together. Gerald handled it so that there wouldn't be a conflict, especially since it was such a top-level position."

"So Kline recommended him for that job?"

She nods. "He did. I know that for an absolute fact."

"Okay. If you're old friends, I'm probably going to get my ass kicked for asking this question, but . . . what are the chances that he would do something unethical? I'm talking about manipulating health data for his own financial benefit, and much worse."

She just about does a double take and looks me right in the eye. "Rico? No chance. Absolutely no chance."

"What did you call him?" I ask, though I know the answer.

"Rico. That was his nickname in high school. Not sure why, but that's what we called him."

"MAYBE we misread the email," Laurie says. "Maybe it's not about drugs at all."

Andy takes the email that Lisa Yates sent to Doris Landry out of his file, and we all read it again:

Lisa: *It's getting worse. Gerald doesn't think that Rico will do anything. I think he's crazy. . . . Rico doesn't just dispense this stuff for nothing. He's a dangerous guy; he's connected to people. I'm afraid to leave my house.*

Doris Landry: *Are you still going to quit your job?*

Lisa: *I think so. I can't live here anymore. If I go somewhere else and get clean, I can start all over. Without Gerald.*

Doris Landry: *You can do it, Lisa. You have strength you don't even realize.*

Lisa: *I'm going to need it.*

"It seems clear to me," I say. "She's talking about drugs."

Andy shakes his head. "Laurie may be right. There are two

references in here which made us think it was drug related. One is 'dispense this stuff' and the other is her comment that she wants to 'get clean.' But what if the stuff he was dispensing was illegal information that they were profiting from? And what if 'get clean' simply meant go straight?"

"I'd like to believe it, but it's a stretch."

"Even in light of what we've learned? There never was any evidence of drug use by either Lisa or Kline; neither autopsy showed any trace of it. And we believe that there is crime, probably informational computer crime, going on at Ardmore. Doesn't this all fit right into that?"

"It does, just not neatly enough for my taste. What does it do for us legally?"

"It helps," Andy says. "One of our best pieces of evidence is the email. We didn't have a Rico to tie it to, but now we do. Will Stephanie Downes testify?"

"You mean to calling him Rico in high school? I would assume so. They were friends, but she's not exactly accusing him of anything. If she resisted and we forced her to come, I don't think she'd lie about it."

"Don't approach her yet," Andy says. "We don't want to take a chance of word getting back to him that we suspect anything."

"Can we force him into a mistake?" Laurie asks.

It's a good question, but I don't have a good answer.

We all agree that we will think about that. For now we will assume that Mahler and probably Jason Musgrove, his boss, are dirty. Unfortunately, in light of our debacle in getting the data from the subpoena, we don't know what they're doing. We just know that they have committed at least three murders to preserve it.

Andy says that he's heading into the den to prepare for tomorrow's court session. Robbie Lillard is going to be Dylan's main witness; he's the homicide detective who worked the case and who arrested me.

"You want me to go over it with you?" I ask.

"No."

"You sure? I know Robbie pretty well; I might be able to help."

"No."

"I'm getting the feeling you don't want my help."

"What tipped you off?" Andy says on the way into the den.

"LIEUTENANT Lillard, you questioned Mr. Douglas at the scene?"

Dylan has painstakingly taken Lillard through his actions that night, starting with the alert he received of the 911 call. Now Dylan's ready to get to the serious stuff.

"I did."

"How did he describe what happened?"

"He said that Mr. Kline had called him and said that he had something to show him, something related to the murder of Lisa Yates. He wouldn't say what it was, just that if Douglas didn't come over, he would give it to the police the next morning."

"Did you ask him why he didn't just let Mr. Kline turn whatever it was over to the police?"

Lillard nods. "Yes. He said that he was working the case, and that it was important to him to know what it was Kline had. He said that he had already spoken to Kline a few days before, and that he had threatened to nail him for the Yates murder."

"What else did Mr. Douglas say?"

"That he and his dog came in and went to the room where the television was on. They assumed Kline was in there. He said they found him dead on the floor."

Dylan uses the opportunity to introduce photos from the scene. They are obviously gory and the jury recoils from them; I'm sure they can't wait to get their own revenge on the animal who did this. Unfortunately, they think that I'm that animal.

"Do these photos accurately reflect the scene in Mr. Kline's house when you arrived?"

"They do. I directed the police photographer myself."

"It was a very bloody scene. Did Mr. Douglas have blood on his clothing?"

"Just some on the bottom of his shoes. He said he went to Mr. Kline's body to feel for a pulse, but there was none."

"At some point, did you tell Mr. Douglas he could leave?"

"Yes, he wrote out a statement and then left. I remained with my officers and with a forensics team. The coroner's office took Mr. Kline's body."

"Did you conduct a search of the area?"

Lillard describes the search and finding bloody clothing and the knife in a plastic garbage bag in a Dumpster, four houses down. DNA tests showed that the blood was Kline's, but that there was a substantial amount of my DNA as well. Kline's blood was also on the knife.

"Were there bloody footprints leading out of the house to the back?"

"Yes. They matched the sneakers found in the garbage bag."

"What did you do next?"

"We obtained and executed a search warrant on Mr. Douglas's house."

"Did you find any other knives similar to the one that you found in the Dumpster?"

Lillard nods. "Yes. The knife matched a set of steak knives that was in his kitchen."

"What about the garbage bag that the knife and clothing were in?"

"There was an open box of garbage bags in Mr. Douglas's house. They were the same make, size, and color as the one in the Dumpster."

Dylan turns Lillard over to Andy for cross-examination. He starts by asking if Lillard recognized me when he arrived at the house.

"I did. I knew Corey . . . Mr. Douglas . . . from his time on the force."

"Did you recognize his dog, Simon?"

"Yes."

"Did Simon have any blood on him?"

"Yes. On his paws."

"When you questioned Mr. Douglas, did you do it in the same room that the body was found in?"

"No, the forensics team was doing their work, so we went into the kitchen."

"Did Simon go with Mr. Douglas into the kitchen?"

"Yes."

"Did he have to be instructed to do that, or did he just go where Mr. Douglas went?"

"He did not have to be instructed."

"When Mr. Douglas finally left, did Simon go with him?"

"Yes."

"Again without being instructed?"

Lillard nods. "Correct."

"When you knew them on the force, was that always the case? To your knowledge, Simon stuck with him at all times?"

"Absolutely."

"Were there bloody paw prints leading to the back of the house, along with the human footprints?"

Lillard seems to fight to resist smiling. "No, there were not."

Andy pauses for a short while to let that sink in on the jury. Then, "Lieutenant, you say you knew Mr. Douglas on the force. At that time, did you consider him a good cop?"

"Very much so."

"A smart cop?"

"Definitely."

"One who understands police procedures and how an investigation is conducted."

"Certainly."

"Would you describe your decision to search the surrounding area as a brilliant one? An inspired one?"

"I'm not sure what you mean."

"Was searching the area standard procedure, or a stroke of genius on your part?"

"It was standard procedure."

"Any good detective would have had it done?"

"Yes."

"So Mr. Douglas, who you just described as a smart cop, would have known a search like that would be standard procedure?"

"I certainly would think so."

"And testing the clothing for DNA, also standard procedure?"

"Yes."

"And obtaining a search warrant for a suspect's house . . . groundbreaking detective work, or standard procedure?"

"Standard procedure."

"So a good cop like Mr. Douglas would likely have known exactly what would be done?"

"I would think so."

"Were you surprised that he left you so many obvious clues?"

"Somewhat . . . yes." I can see Dylan trying not to cringe at this. He's going to be pissed at Lillard for his honesty.

"In the garbage bag, was there a signed note from Mr. Douglas saying, 'Arrest me . . . I did it'?"

Lillard smiles. "I didn't see one."

Andy returns the smile. "So just to recap; please tell me if this accurately sums up the prosecution's view of the situation. Mr. Douglas, smart cop that he was, did not commit the murder and then leave, taking his clothing, knife, and garbage bag with him. Instead, he committed the murder and then stayed there and called the police. He then left all of those items behind, where they could easily be found and traced back to him. Is that about right?"

"I can't speak for the prosecution."

"I think you already have. Thank you, Lieutenant. No further questions."

Andy was brilliant, and I tell him so when he comes back to the defense table.

"Shucks," he says, "enough about me."

What I don't say is what he and I both know. The factual part of today's testimony was squarely on Dylan's side. Andy handled it as well as it could be handled, but the "How could the defendant be this stupid?" defense will rarely carry the day.

We're going to need something more.

LAURIE answered the phone at 10:45 P.M.

Taking the phone into the den where Andy was going over his case notes, she covered up the receiver. "It's for you. He asked if this was the lawyer Andy Carpenter's number. He sounds nervous . . . this is a strange one."

Andy picked up the phone on his desk. "Hello?"

"Mr. Carpenter. My name is Harold Marshall. I have been following the trial. . . . I knew Gerald Kline. Well, let's say I had dealings with him."

"How can I help you, Mr. Marshall?"

"I want to help you, but I do not want my name used. Can I have your word on that?"

"I would need to know what it is you have to say. But I would certainly make every effort."

"If you bring me into it or contact me in any way, I will deny everything."

"I think it would be best for you to say whatever it is you have to say. Then we can go from there."

There was a silence for a few moments, which became a few more. Andy believed the man was trying to decide whether to continue the conversation or abort.

He continued, "I don't think your client killed Gerald Kline. I wanted to kill him myself. I am not without resources."

Andy doesn't say anything; if this guy was going to get to the point, it would have to be at his own pace, on his own terms.

"Kline was blackmailing me; he had information. . . . I could have lost my family, my profession, everything I care about."

"Where did he get this information?"

"I don't know. I had never met him, never had any association with him. He just appeared one day, and everything changed."

"Did you pay him?"

A long pause, then, "Fifty thousand dollars. But it wasn't enough; it was never going to be enough. I was very happy when I read that he was dead. I expected someone else to take his place, but no one did."

"Did Mr. Kline mention anyone else, anyone he was working with?"

"No. Never."

"This was brave of you to come forward."

"I'm not brave at all, and I'm not coming forward. Mr. Carpenter, this is the end of it. I just wanted you to know the truth; maybe you can do something with it."

"Can we meet? Maybe talk about this some more, while preserving your confidentiality?"

"No. Good-bye. Good luck." Click.

As soon as Andy got off the phone, he told Laurie what transpired and then called Sam Willis and Corey Douglas. Andy gave Sam Harold Marshall's name and phone number and asked him to check him out. Andy also asked Sam and Corey to come to his house for a 7:00 A.M. meeting before court, where Sam could share what he'd learned in the interim.

When Andy got off, he asked, "What do you think?"

"Hard to say. I don't usually trust helpful information that comes out of nowhere," Laurie said.

"I don't either, but this one sounded legit, and he sounded scared."

"Let's see what Sam comes up with."

"HAROLD Marshall lives in Pittsburgh. He's forty-eight years old, has been married for twenty-two years, and has two children, one sixteen and the other eleven. He went to Penn State undergrad and med school and is a pediatrician. House is worth $1.6 million, drives an Audi, and both kids are in private school. That's all I've got so far," Sam says.

Andy turns to Laurie and me. "So, what do we think?"

"My instinct is to be skeptical," I say. "But if this person is not real, I don't know what he could have to gain by coming forward."

"Maybe try and change our defense?" Laurie asks.

Andy shakes his head. "He can't do that. We don't have a defense."

I laugh at that in the hope that Andy is joking. Then, "It does fit neatly. Anybody have a guess as to how many records companies like Ardmore have?"

"How many people are there in the country?" Andy says. "Everybody has medical records, and almost all of them would be on file somewhere."

"So hundreds of millions. If the tiniest percentage are people with money who have blackmailable information in there, then the bad guys could make a fortune. It also fits with Lisa's email about Rico, who we think is Richard Mahler. He's dispensing this information to people who are doing the blackmailing and paying him a percentage."

I continue, "Kline was the recruiter. He was screening people that he thought could handle the assignments. It ties together."

"So why kill Kline?" Laurie asks.

"Maybe he was turning on them. Just speculating, but it could have had to do with Lisa Yates's death. Maybe that crossed a line in his mind, and maybe he did have something to show you that night that was a danger to Mahler and whoever else."

"So let's say it's real," Andy says, "mainly because right now we don't have a reason to think it isn't. What do we do with it? And soon, because we're running out of time."

"I think the key is Jason Musgrove. He has to be at the top of this chain, for a few reasons. One, he's the CEO; unless his head is buried in the sand, then he should know what's going on in his company. Two, he's the one who depended on Kline to recommend personnel, most of whom they hired. Three, and most important, it's Musgrove who fired Don Crystal and installed Mahler. That couldn't be a coincidence; they had to have had this planned."

"So?" Laurie asks, obviously hoping that my rambling is leading to a potential course of action.

"So we lean on Mahler to turn on Musgrove. We tell him about Marshall and we threaten to blow the lid on the whole thing in court. He wouldn't know that Marshall won't come forward.

He would assume that if we know about Marshall, then Marshall clearly has made the decision to tell what he knows."

Everybody seems to agree that my plan is either a good idea or a bad idea; nobody knows. The other thing we agree on is that if we do confront Mahler, then Andy should be the one to do it.

As I'm leaving, Andy says, "See you in court. Dylan should be done tomorrow or the next day, and then we're up."

"I guess I should ask you now; are you going to put me on the stand?" I know that defense attorneys hate the idea of their clients testifying.

"I might," he says, surprising me. "Unless I can think of another way."

"Another way to do what?"

"The problem we had at the beginning of the case is still the problem we have now. Your stuff . . . clothing, sneakers, knife . . . were found at the scene. We have no way to explain that, other than you."

"You think the jury will buy my saying I had an instinct my house was broken into, but I didn't notice anything missing and didn't bother to report it?"

He frowns. "I doubt it, but we have nothing else. It is what it is. Juries can't handle a vacuum; if we don't fill it with an explanation, they'll assume that none exists. They might reject ours, but at least it will be there for them to consider."

I turn to leave and then stop. "There's one other thing."

"Not the money again?"

"No, something more important. I want to ask you that, if this goes south, if you would take Simon."

"Of course."

"I don't mean take for your foundation to place in a home. I mean to take him to live out his life here, as a member of your family."

"I know what you meant. And the answer is 'of course.' But I don't think it will be necessary."

"No?"

"No. I think one way or another we are going to win this thing."

TODAY is science and forensics day.

Dylan wants to tie me to the killing beyond a shadow of a doubt, but he also wants an excuse to show the crime scene photos on the big screen again. If a picture is worth a thousand words, a bloody one is worth half a million.

He starts with Janet Carlson, the medical examiner, who testifies that Gerald Kline had his throat slashed and that he therefore bled to death. I know Janet well; I consider her a friend and have worked with her on a number of occasions. She's an outstanding, highly trained medical examiner, but if she were a poorly trained plumbing-supply salesperson, she would still be able to tell that Gerald Kline had his throat slashed and he bled to death.

Andy doesn't question her assessment in his cross-examination; instead he asks her about her experience working with me when I was on the force. She has nothing but praise for my professionalism and says that when she heard I was arrested for the murder, her first reaction was that it couldn't be true.

"Is that still your reaction today?" Andy asks.

"It is," she says, before Dylan can object.

The forensics specialist that Dylan calls is Sergeant Luis Claudio, a twenty-year veteran of the force. I worked with Luis a couple of times, but don't really know him. His reputation is excellent.

Dylan starts with the DNA and spends almost an hour getting Claudio to say that it is absolutely, positively my DNA on the clothing, along with Kline's blood. Claudio quantifies the odds against it as one in a couple of quadrillion; at least that's what I think he says. Anything over a gazillion and I tune out.

I honestly don't think there is a person on the planet who doesn't believe that DNA is ridiculously accurate, so I don't know why prosecutors spend so much time convincing juries of it. I can see the jurors' eyes glazing over as the testimony drones on.

More interesting to them is the blood. That my clothes are saturated with it is interesting to the jurors; they perk up when the subject is raised. Dylan gets Claudio to say that the blood would spurt from the neck wound, making it impossible for a person making the slashing motion to avoid getting it all over him. Because it was a clean cut, Claudio says, it would be even more likely to spurt.

I can tell when Andy starts his cross that he sees potential for us in the blood testimony. "Sergeant Claudio, you testified that it would have been almost impossible for the slasher not to have gotten blood on him or her, is that right?"

"Yes."

"What if the slashing had been done from behind?"

"I was not presented with that hypothetical."

"Mr. Campbell told you that the slasher stood in front of the victim?"

"That was my assumption."

"When did he tell you that? During your coaching session? Did he show you a video of the crime? Maybe we could all see it."

Claudio is annoyed. "I was not coached."

"Wonderful. So let's start over. If the slasher came up behind the victim, grabbed him by the shoulder and slashed across the front, would the slasher's clothes be covered in blood?"

"That would be unlikely."

"Good. Please let me know if I say anything else that contradicts Mr. Campbell's hypothetical."

Dylan objects that Andy is being badgering and argumentative, and since he is, Judge Wallace sustains.

"You said that the blood on the knife found in the Dumpster was Mr. Kline's. Was that the murder weapon?"

"I can't say that for sure."

"So it could have had the blood applied to it, then put in the garbage bag, without having been used to slash Mr. Kline?"

"It's possible."

"You said it was a clean cut, do you remember saying that?"

"Of course."

"Did you examine the knife?"

"Of course."

"It's a serrated-edged kitchen knife. Do they make clean cuts?"

"They can."

"Isn't a serrated edge like a saw, with a jagged blade? Isn't the very purpose of it not to make clean cuts?"

"I can't speak to its purpose; I can only say that the wound could have been made by the knife we are talking about."

Andy finally lets Claudio off the stand, and Dylan calls Sergeant Stew Metosky, another forensics officer who had been on the scene.

"Sergeant Metosky, you checked Mr. Kline's house for fingerprints that night?"

"I did."

"What did you find?"

"Well, obviously Mr. Kline's were everywhere. There were also partial prints from three people that I could not identify, and then I found prints belonging to Mr. Douglas."

"Where were they?"

"Well, there were some in the den, and then there were prints on the outside handle of the back door."

Dylan pretends to be surprised. "He came in through the back door?"

"I have no idea, but he certainly touched the back doorknob."

Andy's cross is quick and to the point. "Sergeant Metosky, you said it was on the outside doorknob of the back door. Was it also on the inside?"

"No."

"Are you aware that there was testimony that the prosecution theory is that Mr. Douglas went out the back, put a garbage bag full of obvious clues in a nearby Dumpster, and then came back in?"

"Yes."

"How did he get out without touching the door?"

"I can't answer that."

"Did you examine the knife for prints?"

"Yes, there were none."

"Which means he filled the bag with clothes containing his own DNA, hoping it would never be found, but took the time to wipe off his prints?"

Dylan objects and Wallace sustains, telling Sergeant Metosky that he doesn't have to answer. I don't think Andy cares; I think the point was to ask the question.

He lets him off the stand, and we're out of here for the day.

Judge Wallace wishes the jury a nice weekend and tells them to be sure it doesn't include media coverage of this trial.

Monday starts our defense.

ANDY has called Richard Mahler four times.

Twice at his office and twice on his cell phone, which Sam tracked down. Sam also set up an app on Andy's phone that would let him record calls that he made or that came in. New Jersey is a one-person-consent state, so he could record any conversation legally. Sam probably wasn't used to doing tech things that are legal, but he seems to have adjusted.

For the two office calls, Andy told the receptionist that it was urgent that he speak to Mr. Mahler, but each time she put him on hold, then came back and said that Mahler was out of the office.

On the cell phone calls, they went to voice mail, and Andy left an urgent message each time. The last one was an implied threat that it was in Mahler's best interests to call Andy back "before it is too late."

Andy's phone rang at noon on Saturday. Caller ID showed that it was Mahler calling, so Andy pressed the button to commence the recording. Then he answered with "Richard Mahler, I'm glad you finally called back."

"Mr. Carpenter, I am going to have to insist that you stop bothering me. I will turn this over to my attorney if I have to. I am not interested in anything you or your client has to say."

"How about Harold Marshall?" Andy asked. "Are you interested in anything he has to say? Because he tells a fascinating story. Actually, not to worry . . . you can read about it in the paper." Andy neglected to mention the part about Marshall vowing never to come forward publicly.

There was dead silence on the phone for at least twenty very long seconds. Then, "I don't know any Harold Marshall."

"It took you all that time to come up with that? That's the best you got?"

"I'm hanging up now."

"You do and you are throwing away your last chance to deal with this. Because the next person you will be talking to about it is a homicide cop. That won't go well for you, Rico."

Another long silence, then, "What do you want?"

"First of all, I want you to know that we know everything. Once Marshall comes forward and they start to turn over more rocks, then everyone will know everything. The only thing we don't know for sure is who is above you. I assume it's Musgrove, but I can't be sure.

"But here's the thing, Rico . . . when something like this goes south, goes public, you don't want to be the top guy. That's a bad place to be. You want to be the guy who identified the top guy. That is the only way to play it, believe me."

"I was a nobody in this. I just did what I was told."

"I know that. But you need to take care of yourself now."

"You don't know Musgrove." Mahler sounded desperate. "He will come after me."

"Not if he's in custody."

There was another long silence, then, "I don't kill people."

"Then you need to tell the police, and my jury, who does."

"I need to think about this. Please give me until tomorrow."

"No longer than that. But understand that it is coming out no matter what. Your only decision is which side to be on."

"I understand."

"Don't blow this one, Rico. You've only got the one shot."

When the call ended, Andy calls me and tells me about his conversation with Mahler, in detail.

"What do you think he will do?" I ask.

"I don't know; he sounded panicked. I know he believed me when I told him we knew everything; mentioning Marshall was the clincher. He should come forward; in these circumstances it would be the smart thing to do. But it could go the other way as well."

"At least we finally know what's going on."

"Tell it to the jury."

I'M not thinking about what will happen if Mahler comes forward.

I'm focused on what will happen if he doesn't.

Andy's threat to blow the lid off this thing, while I hope it seemed credible to Mahler, was actually empty. Without Marshall going public, we have no victims to parade in front of the judge or the public. We know what's going on, but the jury will remain in the dark.

We simply do not have a plan B.

Andy hasn't said so, but plan A is not exactly foolproof either. If Mahler just admitted to the blackmailing, that doesn't clear me of the Kline murder. Mahler would have to identity the real killer, which he might not do. He might not even know who it is; as the computer guy, he could have not been tied in to the violent side of the operation.

I'm sitting in court going nuts agonizing over what Mahler is going to do. Andy, meanwhile, is about to start the defense case.

He clearly has to maintain total concentration; I have no idea how he is able to compartmentalize like this.

His . . . I should say *our* . . . first witness is Cynthia Geisler. Cynthia is a blood spatter expert that Andy has brought in from Chicago.

It must have been an interesting conversation between Cynthia and her parents when they talked about the career path she wanted to follow.

"You're interested in blood?" her mother might have asked. "Isn't that a little ghoulish?"

Cynthia probably laughed. "No, come on, Mom . . . I'm not interested in blood. Blood is creepy. But I am fascinated by how it spatters. Like when the jugular gets slashed."

I'm impressed and grateful to Andy that she is here. I'm sure he could have gotten by without her coming; if he's found something worthwhile for our case in the way the blood spattered, he could have handled it himself. But he didn't; he went the extra mile and brought Geisler in. I'm sure Chicago blood spatter experts do not come cheap.

They may not be cheap, but they're pretty boring. Geisler drones on about how it is unlikely that blood spurting from Kline's neck could have landed in the way that the clothing in the garbage bag appeared. She talks about initial impact, range, and transference, and while she seems to know what she is talking about, I'm not sure the jury is taking it all in.

On cross-examination, Dylan brings the conversation even deeper into the weeds. By the time she is finished on the stand, I think the jury will be ready to take up a collection to send her back to Chicago.

At the first break, Andy checks his phone to see if there are any messages from Mahler. His shake of the head tells me that there aren't any.

After the break, our next witness is Walter Nichols. He's the neighbor who called 911 to report the domestic violence incident that night, which now seems like ten years ago. I could argue that Nichols is the cause of everything that has happened since; certainly if he hadn't made that call, I wouldn't be sitting in a courtroom wearing a GPS ankle bracelet.

Andy is taking an interesting approach here. My talking to Nichols in the first place supports Dylan's position on my motive, that I was out to get Kline out of my guilt at not doing more the night I was called to the house.

Andy's belief is that since the jury already heard testimony about it, and it happens to be true, we should embrace it. We should show it as evidence of my inherent goodness in wanting to protect Lisa, and my desire to see justice done after she died.

Legal, by the book, no violent vendetta, justice.

Andy takes him through the original night, what he heard, and why he called. Andy pays particular attention to Nichols claiming that he heard Kline say, "You'll do what you're told."

"Did you know what he was referring to?" Andy asks. "Do you know what he was saying she was told?"

"No."

"Could it have had to do with something outside of their domestic situation?"

"I suppose so."

On cross, Dylan tries to make it seem as if I was obsessed with Kline. Nichols, to his credit, is not going along with it. He says I was just asking questions about that night, and that he didn't get the feeling I was intent on any kind of revenge.

Lunch brings two more times that Andy checks for messages, with the same result.

"He would have called if he was going to," I say, and Andy nods his agreement.

Laurie joins us for lunch because she is going to be our next witness. It is rare that Andy calls on her in this capacity, but in this case she is easily the best one to get certain points across. We don't talk about her testimony; I'm sure she and Andy have gone over it as much as they need to. And we also don't talk much about Mahler; all of us feel the same sense of dread that our plan has not worked.

When Laurie takes the stand, Andy asks her what her occupation is. She says private investigator and confirms that she has been working for the defense team.

He introduces Lisa Yates's phone records, which we have legally subpoenaed, and which match the ones that Sam had obtained through other-than-legal means.

"When we looked at these records together, did we notice anything that we found of particular interest?"

Dylan is out of his chair and objecting to this testimony as not being even "tangentially relevant" to the case we are trying.

Judge Wallace calls the lawyers to a bench conference so they can discuss it out of earshot of the jury. I can't hear what they are saying, but I'm sure that Andy is explaining that Dylan opened the door to testimony about Lisa Yates's death by trying to set up my motive.

I assume that works, because the lawyers leave the bench and Andy continues his questioning. He asks what about the bill caught Laurie's eye, and she mentions the repeated calls from Lisa to Jana Mitchell. Most notable was the forty-five-minute call the night before Lisa was killed.

"It wasn't stunning news," Laurie said, "and it could have just been that they were friends talking. But it was significant enough to get me to call Jana Mitchell and ask her about it."

"And did you?"

"Yes. She was friendly enough, but as soon as I asked her about

Lisa Yates, she seemed to get fearful. She even denied knowing Lisa. Almost immediately after that she hung up on me."

"So what did you do?"

"Well, it was such an unusual reaction that it piqued my interest. So I flew out to Cincinnati the next day to try and get her to talk to me, to tell me anything that she might know about Lisa Yates."

"And did you do that?"

"Yes. I flew there the next afternoon, had dinner, and went to her home at around eight thirty."

"Did you speak to her?"

"No."

"Why not?"

"She was murdered in her home ninety minutes before I got there."

I can see the jury react in surprise to Laurie's statement.

"Did you consider it a coincidence that Ms. Mitchell was murdered the day after appearing frightened by your talking about Lisa Yates?"

"I did not. I felt, and will always feel, guilt that I did or said something that ultimately led to her being murdered."

"Thank you. No further questions."

Dylan's cross-examination does not attack the accuracy of Laurie's testimony. She related a series of events that are obviously true, and that she lived through. Instead he asks if she has any evidence that any of this is related to the death of Gerald Kline.

"I can't prove that it is, no," Laurie says.

"I didn't ask if you could prove it," Dylan says. "I asked if you have evidence of a connection that you can present to this court."

"I do not. But we're getting there."

Dylan could object and ask the judge to strike the last comment, but he's smart enough to know that the jury has already heard it. So instead he just smiles condescendingly and says, "Please let us know when you do."

Laurie leaves the stand and exits the courtroom as the judge gives the standard spiel to the jury to not talk to anyone about the case or let themselves be exposed to media coverage.

When he's finished and the jury has been dismissed, we turn to leave as well. As we reach the rear door, Laurie is coming back in. The look on her face causes Andy to ask, "What's the matter?"

"Richard Mahler hanged himself this morning. His housekeeper discovered the body."

I have no idea if Richard Mahler really hanged himself.

He could certainly have been murdered, and it was then intentionally made to look like a suicide. The way this case has gone, that would certainly not be a shocker. But I am certain of one thing, and that is that he's dead.

Laurie makes a couple of calls to friends on the force who are in positions to know. They say that the prevailing wisdom is that Mahler did, in fact, commit suicide and even left a brief note.

I call Janet Carlson, the medical examiner who testified as one of Dylan's witnesses.

"Hi, Corey. Sorry about testifying like that; I really had no choice."

"Not to worry, Janet. It's your job and you told the truth. No problem with that."

"I shouldn't have to tell you this, but I think the charge against you is a bag of horseshit."

I laugh. "Thanks, Janet. You're a delicate flower."

She returns the laugh. "So I've been told. What can I do for you?"

"Richard Mahler. Are you calling it a suicide?"

"Between us? Because I have not discussed it with anyone yet."

"Just me, Laurie, and Andy."

"Good enough. I'm calling it a suicide because I have no reason not to. All the signs are there, but in these cases you never know."

"What did the note say?"

"Short and to the point: 'I'm so sorry for what I've done.' That's it."

I thank her and renew my promise to keep it confidential until she releases her report.

Maybe Andy will feel differently, but to me the manner of his death doesn't seem terribly consequential to our case. Either way, it effectively closes the door to any possibility we have to reveal the conspiracy during our trial. The jury is not going to hear about the blackmail scheme that Gerald Kline was a player in because we simply have no evidence to present to them.

Mahler's death fits in, I hope, with the defense Andy is going to offer, that Gerald Kline's death was just one in a series of violent, chaotic events that have surrounded Ardmore and consumed everybody that Kline and Lisa Yates were involved in.

If the jury buys into it, then they will, I hope, be able to see that I have not been a player in that, and that I was clearly not in a position to have committed these other murders.

Laurie has a different idea. "I'm going to Pittsburgh."

"Why would you do that?"

"To talk to Harold Marshall. To get him to reconsider and

come forward with his story. Tied into the Mahler suicide, it would be powerful stuff."

Andy shakes his head. "This time you go with Marcus. Cincinnati didn't work out so well; we want to make sure Pittsburgh isn't worse."

"No chance. I can handle myself. And we want to cajole this guy, not scare the hell out of him."

"He told me that if we come for him, he'll deny everything."

Laurie nods. "And maybe he will. But maybe not. It's certainly worth a try. And you and Ricky can have another boys' night."

"How much pizza can we eat?"

So Laurie once again books her flight for first thing the next morning. I'm not optimistic that she'll have any success in convincing Marshall; Andy had said he was adamant that he be left out of it. But like she says, it's worth a try, and I appreciate her making the effort.

But I think our fate, my fate, is going to be determined in court.

One way or the other.

"CAPTAIN Stanton, if you know, who is Jake Gardener?" Andy asks.

Pete looks uncomfortable; he's not used to testifying as part of a defense case. I know that discomfort is tempered somewhat by the fact that he is helping me, and I appreciate that.

"He is, or was, a contract killer."

"You said 'he was.' Does that mean he has changed occupations or is deceased?"

"He is deceased."

Andy acts surprised. "How and when did he die?"

"He was killed in a downtown Paterson parking lot almost four weeks ago."

"Has that crime been solved?"

"Not yet; we are working some leads, but nothing solid." Pete is lying; there is no way they have any leads, and he must be pissed because he is certain that Andy and Marcus are somehow involved in Gardener's death.

"When the body was discovered, were any possessions he was carrying confiscated?"

"Yes."

"Including a weapon?"

"Yes."

"What about a cell phone?"

"Yes."

Andy introduces as evidence the GPS record from that cell phone, which we again subpoenaed after Sam had already provided it to us. Andy asks Pete to identify it and he does.

Then Andy points to the night of Kline's murder and gets Pete to say that the phone was in Kline's house an hour before I called the police to the house and reported Kline's death.

"So the phone was definitely there?"

Pete nods. "According to these records."

"So just to be clear, a man you personally believe is a contract killer was in Gerald Kline's house that night?"

"Apparently so."

This is significant evidence, and I'm sure that Dylan considers it essential that he challenge it. He does that on his cross-examination.

"Captain Stanton, you said that Jake Gardener was a contract killer. How many murders did he commit?"

"I don't have the exact number."

"Fair enough. How many murders was he convicted of?"

"He was never convicted of a murder. He was convicted of other crimes. He—"

Dylan interrupts. "Never convicted? So apparently in your mind he was exempt from the innocent-until-proven-guilty thing that happens to be in the Constitution. Let's try it another way. How many murders was he charged with?"

"He was never charged."

"So he never went before a jury like this one, to be judged on whether he was an actual killer?"

"That's correct."

"So this is a contract killer who was never charged, never convicted, and you have no idea who he killed. Captain Stanton, have you encountered a good number of contract killers in your career?"

"Unfortunately, yes."

"Is it not their style to do the deed and then leave?"

"What do you mean?"

"Do they generally set up an elaborate scam to frame someone else?"

"Not in my experience."

"Was there ever any allegation that Mr. Gardener had done such a thing before?"

"Not that I am aware of."

"These records allegedly say that Mr. Gardener's phone was there? Do you know who was carrying it?"

"I do not."

"Do these records show where Mr. Gardener was that night?"

"They do not."

"So just to recap, what we know is that the phone of a person never even charged with a homicide was at Mr. Kline's house well before Mr. Douglas arrived? Is that accurate?"

"It is."

"Thank you."

Andy tells Judge Wallace that we are letting Pete off the stand subject to recall later on.

Mercifully, the judge adjourns court early because one of

the jurors has a medical issue. The judge tells Andy and Dylan that if it is not resolved today, he will have to move in one of the alternate jurors as a replacement. Andy seems unconcerned with that; he has no idea whether that particular juror, or the alternate, is favorable to our side.

I go back to Andy's to pick up copies of trial material that I can go over and most likely get nowhere with. I get there before he does because he has to pick up Ricky at his friend Will Rubenstein's house.

When Andy arrives, he starts to gather copies of the documents for me and also texts me a copy of the recording he made of the phone call from Mahler. I hadn't heard it, but want to.

As he is doing this, Laurie calls. They speak briefly, then Andy says, "Hold on, let me put this on the speaker so Corey can hear it." He does so. "Start over."

Laurie's voice comes through the speaker. "I went to Harold Marshall's office; he's a pediatrician. I told the receptionist that I was a private investigator and had to speak to him about a very important matter. So I sat for a half hour in the waiting room with a bunch of coughing and sneezing five-year-olds. I'll be bringing those germs home with me."

"Sounds like fun," Andy says.

"It was. I was finally brought back to his office, and I told him why I was there. He claimed to have absolutely no idea what I was talking about."

Andy nods. "He said he would deny it."

"Well, he did a hell of a job denying it. He seemed bewildered and said I must have the wrong Harold Marshall. I confirmed his cell phone number and he started to act worried. He asked if he should call the police, that someone was out there impersonating him."

"So you believed him?" I asked.

"I did. If he was lying, he's the Brando of pediatricians."

I don't know what to make of Laurie's talk with Harold Marshall.

I've been thinking about it all afternoon and basically getting nowhere. After dinner I talk about it with Dani; she's become a frequent sounding board for me. It's good to have someone to talk to other than Simon, someone who doesn't fake looking interested in the hope of getting a biscuit.

"There are two ways of looking at it," I say. "One is that Marshall was lying, that he's just a good actor. He told Andy that if we tried to contact him, he would deny everything, and that's what he did. That probably makes the most sense, despite Laurie's feeling about it."

"Then we're back to where we started," Dani says. "No way to bring in the blackmail scam."

"Right. The other way to think about it is that Laurie was right. Marshall wasn't lying; he truly had no idea what she was talking about it. His denial was real."

"Where does that leave us?"

"That somebody is pulling the strings and has been pulling them all along. And that the whole idea of blackmail is wrong, that it was an attempt to lead us in the wrong direction."

"A successful attempt."

"For sure. We've been on the other end of those strings since the beginning. They keep leading us to dead ends. We are going where we're told to go, and when we arrive, there's nothing there."

"So if it's not blackmail, then it's something else."

"Which brings us back to square one. We've never been able to figure out what that something else is. If we have that, we'll have everything. But we're no closer to knowing that than we were at the beginning."

"What about Richard Mahler?" Dani asks. "If Marshall wasn't really part of a blackmail scheme, then why did he panic the way he did when Andy threatened him? Why did he commit suicide? And was he really the Rico that Lisa Yates referred to in that email?"

Those are all excellent questions, and I hadn't thought of them. "To quote Chris Berman of ESPN," I say, "'Let's go to the tape.'"

I take out my phone and play the conversation that Andy had with Mahler. Neither Dani nor I had heard it before.

Mahler: *"Mr. Carpenter, I am going to have to insist that you stop bothering me. I will turn this over to my attorney if I have to. I am not interested in anything you or your client has to say."*

Andy: *"How about Harold Marshall? Are you interested in anything he has to say? Because he tells a fascinating story. Actually, not to worry . . . you can read about it in the paper."*

Mahler: *"I don't know any Harold Marshall."*

Andy: *"It took you all that time to come up with that? That's the best you got?"*

Mahler: *"I'm hanging up now."*

Andy: *"You do and you are throwing away your last chance to deal with this. Because the next person you will be talking to about it is a homicide cop. That won't go well for you, Rico."*

Mahler: *"What do you want?"*

Andy: *"First of all, I want you to know that we know everything. Once Marshall comes forward and they start to turn over more rocks, then everyone will know everything. The only thing we don't know for sure is who is above you. I assume it's Musgrove, but I can't be sure. But here's the thing, Rico . . . when something like this goes south, goes public, you don't want to be the top guy. That's a bad place to be. You want to be the guy who identified the top guy. That is the only way to play it, believe me."*

Mahler: *"I was a nobody in this. I just did what I was told."*

Andy: *"I know that. But you need to take care of yourself now."*

Mahler: *"You don't know Musgrove. He will come after me."*

Andy: *"Not if he's in custody."*

Mahler: *"I don't kill people."*

Andy: *"Then you need to tell the police, and my jury, who does."*

Mahler: *"I need to think about this. Please give me until tomorrow."*

Andy: *"No longer than that. But understand that it is coming out no matter what. Your only decision is which side to be on."*

Mahler: *"I understand."*

Andy: *"Don't blow this one, Rico. You've only got the one shot."*

When the tape is finished, I say, "I want to play this again." So I do, listening carefully to every word Mahler says.

When we've heard it for the second time, Dani says, "Maybe it wasn't Harold Marshall that Mahler was worried about. He says he never heard of Marshall. Maybe he was reacting to Andy calling him 'Rico.' It wasn't until he heard that that he started to sound worried."

"That doesn't matter."

"Why not?"

"Because that voice on the call . . . that wasn't Richard Mahler."

I can tell that Andy has doubts that I'm right about the Mahler phone call.

I only met with Mahler once, and voices can sound different over the phone than in person. But I'm good with voices, and I am 100 percent positive that I am right. Well, maybe 90 percent. Or 80.

If I am right, and it wasn't Mahler on the phone, then he was murdered. Pure and simple. There is no other credible explanation for his death.

I suspect we can find a number of other people who were closer to Mahler that could confirm or deny his voice. But there is time for that later; right now we have to figure out what it means, and how it can help us . . . how it can help me. I am officially a self-centered defendant.

I mentally go back over all the times we thought we had something and were thwarted. One thing that sticks out in my mind is

Steven Landry. Andy and I thought he was lying to us when we talked to him about his mother, Doris. She had been the person Lisa Yates emailed about her fear of Rico, and whose obituary was one of three in her suitcase.

When I called him back to ask about his mother's friends, all of whom he said he had contacted to inform them of her death, he got belligerent and refused to help. That has bugged me periodically, but I never followed up on it.

Now is as good a time as any.

I call Sam first thing in the morning. "Sam, can you access Doris Landry's email account? I want to know who some of her friends were . . . who were the people she emailed most often. We know that Lisa Yates was one of them, but who were the others?"

"No problem," Sam says, as usual.

"I'll be in court. Just call me when you have something; I'll get your message and call you back."

"Will do."

When I get to court, Andy seems to be taking my claim that it wasn't Mahler on the call more seriously, or at least he's contemplating what it might mean if I am right.

"We still don't know what's going on . . . where they're making their money," he says. "But if that wasn't Mahler, then it means he was murdered, and it means they're cleaning up all the loose ends."

"I agree, and Jason Musgrove is the last one standing."

"The last one that we know about. Musgrove might be a lying piece of garbage and a total thief, but I'm not sure he has the connections or guts to be arranging all this violence."

I tell Andy about my instructions to Sam about Doris Landry's emails, and he approves. "If we throw enough crap against the wall," he says, "we might get something that sticks." It's an interesting legal strategy.

Today our defense will focus on the attempt by Carlos Evaldi
to murder me in my home. To tell the story, Andy calls Lieutenant
Scott Leeman, a homicide detective who was with Pete Stanton
when they arrived at the house that night. Andy could have had
Pete tell the story as part of his earlier testimony, but Andy felt
that the more respected cops that testify during the defense case,
the better. He also plans to recall Pete later on a different subject.

After setting up that Dani called 911, Andy asks Lieutenant
Leeman what they found when they arrived at the house that
night.

"A man named Carlos Evaldi was in Mr. Douglas's bedroom.
He was deceased, having been shot once in the head. A gun was
still in his hand."

Dylan predictably objects and asks for a conference. This time
Judge Wallace sends the jury out and hears arguments in open
court. I'm glad about that, because it means I can hear it.

"Your Honor, Mr. Carpenter is conducting a fishing expedi-
tion on a scale that I personally have never seen before. Are we
going to hear about every murder ever committed? Nicole Brown
and Ron Goldman? Sharon Tate? Unless and until Mr. Carpenter
makes a showing otherwise, they have as much to do with the case
we are trying as Carlos Evaldi."

Andy shakes his head as if saddened by what he is hearing.
"Your Honor, Mr. Douglas was actively investigating the murders of both Lisa Yates and Gerald Kline. It is a fair inference to
draw that this was an attempt to stop those investigations in their
tracks.

"The larger point is that people related to this case have been
dropping like flies: the murders have been piling up since day one.
The jury has a right to know about them and to decide whether
it makes sense to pluck Mr. Douglas out of the chaos and charge
him."

Judge Wallace has gone too far down this road to make a U-turn now. He allows the witness, with a half-hearted admonition to Andy that he needs to demonstrate relevance.

The jury is called in again, and Andy goes back to questioning Lieutenant Leeman. "Had any other shots been fired?"

"Yes. There were three bullets fired into pillows on the bed. They had obviously been placed that way to make it appear that Mr. Douglas was sleeping in it."

"Were you able to determine how Mr. Evaldi entered the premises?"

"He disabled the burglar alarm and entered through a rear door."

"Does that take expertise?" Andy asks.

"Considerable. This was clearly not a novice at work."

"Was Mr. Evaldi known to law enforcement?"

"Yes. He had served two jail terms, one for manslaughter. He was commonly considered a hired gun."

"Was there anyone else in the house?"

"Yes, a Ms. Dani Kendall. She said that when Mr. Douglas's dog alerted them to the intruder, Mr. Douglas instructed her to go into the closet with the phone to call nine-one-one. She did so and was in there when the shooting took place."

Andy turns Lieutenant Leeman over to Dylan, who appears to shrug Leeman's testimony off as unimportant to the matter at hand. "Lieutenant, can we assume you conducted an investigation of this incident?"

"Of course. It is ongoing."

"Good. Have you discovered in your ongoing investigation anything that connects this incident to the murder of Gerald Kline?"

"Not so far."

"Nothing at all?" Dylan asks, pressing the point.

"No."

"Lieutenant, how many years have you been on the police force?"

"Next month will be twelve years."

"Thank you for your service. There has been testimony that Mr. Douglas was on the force for twenty-five years."

"I believe that's correct," Leeman says, though he wasn't asked a question.

"Have you made enemies in your twelve years? I'm talking about criminals, perhaps those you've arrested?"

"Of course."

"Some of them violent criminals?"

"Of course."

"That's par for the course, isn't it? For a cop who has served twelve years, like yourself, or even more so for one who has served twenty-five, like Mr. Douglas. The more years you serve, the more arrests you make, the more enemies you have?"

"I can't speak for Mr. Douglas."

Dylan smiles. "I'm not asking you to. Would you be shocked if someone tried to exact revenge on you for something you've done in your capacity as a police officer?"

"I try to guard against it."

"As Mr. Douglas did when he shot Mr. Evaldi?"

"I don't know Mr. Evaldi's motivation, whether he was looking for revenge or had a different motive entirely. As I said, it's under investigation."

"Thank you, Lieutenant. Good luck with your investigation."

During the break, I check my messages and there is one from Sam asking that I call him back.

The first thing he says when he gets on the phone is "Doris Landry's email account has been wiped clean."

"What does that mean?"

"The account still exists, but there are no longer any emails there. They would be somewhere on the provider's server, but there's no way for me to access them."

"Who could have wiped it?"

"Anyone with the password. Her son had it, right?"

"Apparently so," I say.

"So it could have been him."

"Sam, I need you to do something else. It's a big ask. . . . Do you mind?"

"Are you kidding? I love this stuff. You know, I'm licensed to carry."

"I don't think there will be any shooting. But I need you to go down to Somers Point and locate some friends of Doris Landry. Get their contact information, phone numbers, and find one or more who are willing to talk to me. Can you do it first thing in the morning?"

"Of course. You want me to call you from down there with the names?"

"If you get any." I don't say so, but I don't think there is a chance in hell that he will get any names. I don't think Doris Landry had any friends.

"IT'S decision time," Andy says, and I know what he means.

We are almost at the end of the defense case, and we need to decide whether I am going to testify. I want to tell my story, but I also trust Andy's instincts and expertise in this situation more than my own. "What do you think?" I ask.

"The positive is that you could explain how your clothing and knife got on the scene. It's not a terribly credible explanation, even though it's true. But it fills in a blank that the jury must be wondering about.

"The negatives are that your explanation, and everything else you say, will be viewed as self-serving. And there is really no information that you have, other than the clothing and knife, that we haven't already gotten in. And of course the big problem is that you would be exposed to cross-examination."

"It would not be my first time on the stand."

"I'm aware of that." He's kind enough not to mention that he once manhandled me on a cross-examination; that could now be factoring into his decision.

"So bottom line?" I ask.

"I don't think you should do it. I think we're muddying the water enough to at least get a hung jury. But I obviously could be wrong. And it's your call, one hundred percent. If you want to tell your story, I will help you tell it."

"No, I trust your judgment. I won't testify." Then, "I'm anxious to hear from Sam from down in Somers Point."

Andy nods. "I understand. But you could be surprised again. He might come back with her entire mah-jongg team."

"I don't think so."

"Either way, let's not count on solving the crime before the end of the trial because it's not likely to happen. Let's focus on getting twelve not-guilty votes."

Andy calls Stephanie Downes, Gerald Kline's partner, to the stand. Her testimony is quick and targeted. He gets her to tell the jury that she went to high school with Richard Mahler, that Kline recommended him, and that he went on to be the top computer guy at Ardmore. Most important, she mentions that in high school Mahler's nickname was Rico.

There is no mention of Mahler's death in her direct testimony, and because her testimony has done no damage to Dylan's case, he asks no questions in cross-examination.

Next Andy recalls Pete Stanton. He introduces as evidence the email sent by Lisa Yates to Doris Landry. "Captain Stanton, could you read this part of it to the jury, please."

Pete reads the words of Doris Landry: "'I'm afraid to ask. But is there anything new with your situation?'"

Andy then asks Pete to read Lisa Yates's words in response, which he does: "'It's getting worse. Gerald doesn't think that Rico will do anything. I think he's crazy. . . . Rico doesn't just dispense this stuff for nothing. He's a dangerous guy; he's connected to people. I'm afraid to leave my house.'"

"Based on this email, written not long before her death, would you say that Lisa Yates believed she was in danger, physical danger, from someone named Rico?"

Pete nods. "I would, yes."

"And would you also say that Lisa believed someone named Gerald was involved in this, and in danger himself, also from someone named Rico?"

"Yes."

"During the course of your investigation of this case, have you encountered another Gerald besides Gerald Kline?"

"No."

"Captain Stanton, are you aware of earlier testimony by Stephanie Downes saying that Richard Mahler's nickname was Rico? That he was called that going back to high school?"

"I am."

"During the course of your investigation of this case, have you encountered another person named or nicknamed Rico besides Richard Mahler?"

"No, I have not."

"Captain Stanton, based on this information, will you be interviewing Richard Mahler?"

"No."

"Why not?"

"He's dead. He was found hanged in his home a few days ago. The death was ruled by the medical examiner as a suicide, but the investigation is ongoing."

"Thank you. No further questions."

Dylan gets up quickly, intent on cleaning up the mess that Andy created for him. "Captain, let's read the email again, if you don't mind." Dylan points to the paper. "This paragraph will suffice."

Pete reads, "'It's getting worse. Gerald doesn't think that Rico will do anything. I think he's crazy. . . . Rico doesn't just dispense this stuff for nothing. He's a dangerous guy; he's connected to people. I'm afraid to leave my house.'"

"After you read this the first time, you said that it meant that Lisa Yates was saying that Gerald, whoever he might be, was in danger. Can you tell us where in the email it says that?"

"It's an inference I made."

"Ah, an inference. For the purpose of this part of your testimony, can you just stick to the facts?"

Andy objects that Dylan is badgering the witness, and Judge Wallace sustains. Dylan then asks, "Is there anything in there that says that Gerald is in danger?"

"Not specifically, no."

"And either way, this would be Lisa Yates's opinion, correct?"

"Correct."

"You said that you were not aware of other Geralds in this investigation, correct?"

"Yes."

"Is it possible that she was not referring to Gerald Kline?"

"Possible. I consider it unlikely."

"Do you know how many Geralds there are in the United States?"

"I have no idea."

"Would you be surprised if I told you that census records list more than five hundred and fourteen thousand people named Gerald?"

"I told you I had no idea; therefore I wouldn't be surprised."

"As long as we're talking about things for which you have no idea, do you know why Richard Mahler committed suicide?"

"No."

"To your knowledge, was Richard Mahler in the house the night Gerald Kline was killed?"

"I don't know."

"Do you know how Richard Mahler might have come into possession of Mr. Douglas's clothing and kitchen knife?"

"I don't."

"Thank you."

Judge Wallace turns to Andy to see if he has any more witnesses to call. I almost want to grab him and say that I changed my mind, and that I insist on testifying, but I don't.

So all I do is listen as Andy says five of the scariest words I've ever heard: "Your Honor, the defense rests."

"I can't find anyone who knows her," Sam says.

He's calling me on the way home from Somers Point and reporting on his quest to connect me with friends of Doris Landry's.

This is exactly what I was expecting. "You asked her neighbors?"

"I did my best. Her house is empty; somebody obviously cleared it out. But the whole neighborhood is mostly abandoned; they're going to be knocking it all down to put in an extension on a highway. So there aren't many people left, and the ones who are still there have no idea who I am talking about."

"Okay. Thanks for trying, Sam."

"When I get back, I can do more research . . . maybe access her phone records."

"Not necessary. I'll take it from here."

When we get off the phone, I call Andy. Laurie gets on the extension, and I tell them about my conversation with Sam.

"So you think this proves your theory?" Laurie asks.

"Absolutely. One hundred percent."

"You have a tendency toward overconfidence," Andy says. "You think you can handle this from here?"

"With my teammates? One hundred percent."

"There's that overconfidence again."

"It's part of my charm."

I get off the phone and call Don Crystal, my pajama-wearing, Tang-drinking buddy. Like last time, he answers with "Yo."

"You ready to help bring down Jason Musgrove?" I ask.

"What do you mean 'bring down'?"

"Send to jail, destroy . . . think of it in those terms."

"Man, if that's what you're talking about, you don't even have to buy me a meal." Then Crystal adds, "Unless you want to."

"When this is over, it's all-you-can-eat."

"Just point me in the right direction."

"Okay, there will be more, but start with this. You were right; it's an insurance scam. You got a pen?"

"Hold on." Then, "Okay, go ahead."

"There are three people. Doris Landry of Somers Point, New Jersey; Samuel Devers, of Springfield, Massachusetts; and Eric Seaver of Brunswick, Maine. I want to know what insurance companies Ardmore sent their medical information to."

"I don't work there anymore. I can't get into their system."

"Bullshit. You can get in."

He pauses for a few moments. "Yeah, I can get in. Just keep it between us. It ain't legal."

"That's okay. What Musgrove did ain't legal either. Get back to me when you have the information. But soon."

DYLAN stands to make his closing argument.

He pauses as if to show the heavy weight that his words will carry, so he wants to choose his words carefully. My guess is he has rehearsed every word of it and only wants it to appear spontaneous and heartfelt.

"Ladies and gentlemen, I've participated in a lot of trials. They have included a lot of different charges against defendants from all walks of life. Some of those trials have been quick, and some have dragged on endlessly. And to be honest, I've won some and I've lost some.

"But this trial has been unusual in one important regard. You've sat through a lot of testimony by many witnesses, yet nothing has changed. Let me repeat that . . . nothing has changed.

"Right at the beginning, you learned that Corey Douglas was in Gerald Kline's house that fateful night. You learned that he carried a grudge against Mr. Kline; he voiced it repeatedly, even to a police officer. You learned that Mr. Douglas's blood-soaked clothing and knife were hidden in a Dumpster four houses down from Mr. Kline's house.

"You learned all that at the outset of the trial, and you know what? It's all still true. And you know what else? You have not heard an explanation from the defense for any of it.

"They have tried to distract you with stories of other deaths, none of which have anything to do with the murder of Gerald Kline. Have they identified anyone else besides Mr. Douglas who had a vendetta against Mr. Kline? Have they identified anyone else besides Mr. Douglas who had a motive to kill him?

"Have they identified anyone else whose bloodstained clothing and knife were found near the scene? No, but by all means, they want you to clear Mr. Douglas of this crime because someone else murdered someone else.

"It's crazy. Was Lee Harvey Oswald innocent because someone else murdered Martin Luther King? That is literally the logic behind the defense position.

"Don't be fooled by all of the smoke and mirrors. Focus on the facts . . . on the access, on the motive, and on the evidence. That is all you need; it tells you all you have to know to make the correct decision.

"Thank you."

Andy wastes no time getting up; he starts speaking at the very moment that Judge Wallace invites him to do so.

"Ladies and gentlemen, I would respectfully disagree with Mr. Campbell. Because in my view one thing is certain, and that is that everything has changed.

"At the beginning of the trial, Mr. Kline seemed to be a successful entrepreneur who was tragically murdered. And let me make one thing clear: that murder, like all violent deaths, was and is tragic.

"But since then, you have learned that he lived in a dangerous world, surrounded by chaos and, yes, death. You have learned that a phone belonging to Jake Gardener, a man identified by the man in charge of the Homicide Division of the Paterson Police Department as a contract killer, was in Gerald Kline's house an hour before his body was discovered.

"Mr. Campbell implied that perhaps the phone was there but that Mr. Gardener was not. Does it seem logical to you that Gardener lent someone his phone to go to Mr. Kline's house and then took it back? Because Mr. Gardener had it in his possession when his own body was discovered.

"You've learned that Lisa Yates, a very close friend of Mr. Kline, was also murdered. You saw an email she wrote in which she expressed worry for her own safety from someone named Rico, and which included Mr. Kline commenting on Rico's potential dangerousness. And you've learned that Rico, Richard Mahler, has himself recently died by violent means, possibly suicide, possibly not.

"You've learned that Mr. Douglas, while investigating this case, was the target of still another contract killer. He was able to thwart the attack and kill the intruder. Is it reasonable to consider it possible that the purpose of the killer was to abort the investigation? I think so.

"I don't know for sure how Mr. Douglas's clothing and knife happened to wind up in that Dumpster. But I can tell you this. When I left for court this morning, I did not lock my sweatpants and kitchen utensils in a safe. Did you? When I get home each night, I would not notice if a sweatshirt and knife were missing. Would you?

"But the prosecution would have you believe that Mr. Douglas, a savvy police officer of twenty-five years, hid incriminating evidence where he had to know it would be found. Then he called the police to the scene and waited for them to arrive.

"Let me ask you this: Why wouldn't he have just left, taking that incriminating evidence with him? Why do everything to call attention to himself, to make himself the obvious suspect, if he didn't have to? Do his actions make any sense at all? Would such a smart cop become such a stupid criminal?

"Ladies and gentlemen, I would submit that not only has the prosecution's reasonable doubt threshold not been met, it hasn't even been approached. Corey Douglas served this community well and heroically for twenty-five years. He has done nothing wrong. At the very least, we owe him our thanks and his freedom."

Andy comes back and sits next to me at the defense table. I lean over, offer my hand, and as we shake hands, I say, "You were worth every penny."

I have never experienced anything like this . . . not even close.

I'm not sure too many people have.

It's been thirty-six hours since Judge Wallace sent twelve strangers into a room to decide whether I will spend most or all of the rest of my life in prison. Neither Andy nor I have any idea what is going on in that room, and we will not know until they have made their final decision.

Andy refuses to make a prediction and does not even want to talk about it. He has about half a million weird superstitions that he observes during a verdict watch, and pretty much everything I say violates one of them, so we don't discuss it at all.

Today is Saturday, but the jury has been sequestered, and the plan is to deliberate through the entire weekend, or less if they reach their verdict.

Andy is very much aware, as is Laurie, of the other major pressure that I am experiencing. I am in a race to break open the conspiracy that has been going on at Ardmore. There is no time to wait; if I don't act quickly, then it will be impossible to accomplish. It will literally disappear; that is the very nature of it.

But if I am found guilty, I will go to prison for a time, no matter what I am able to accomplish at Ardmore. The justice system moves slowly, and possibly not at all.

Don Crystal has gotten back to me with the information on the three people I asked about, Landry, Devers, and Seaver. He is awaiting further instructions.

I have talked to the people I need to talk to, and everything is arranged as well as it can be.

So all is in place.

Today is the day.

I make the phone calls necessary to start the process and to confirm that Jason Musgrove and Stephanie Downes are at their respective homes. I'm about to take the next step when Andy calls. His three words cause my heart to start pounding in my chest.

"There's a verdict."

He tells me that we need to be in court in forty-five minutes, and that he'll meet me at the courthouse.

"I can't be there, Andy." He has to know why I am saying this since Laurie has already left their house to get into position.

"You can't be there to hear your own verdict?" he says, incredulous.

"No. I really can't. You know that."

"Judge Wallace will be beyond pissed off. He's got this little idiosyncrasy about him: when he tells the defendant to rise, he likes the defendant to actually be in the courtroom."

"Sorry. Andy, I gotta go. There's no other way."

"I'll cover for you. Just be careful. Be really careful."

The drive to Jason Musgrove's house takes about twenty minutes. Simon is in the back seat. I think he senses something is up; he sits up straight when we're working. He probably doesn't have a role to play here, but since he's been involved throughout, I feel like I owe it to him for him to be around for the resolution.

I pull into the driveway. I don't want to hide; I want it to be obvious to anyone interested that I'm here.

I ring the bell and he answers the door. I'm glad he lives alone; if he had a wife here, it would complicate matters greatly. It wouldn't make this impossible, but it would make it more difficult.

It takes a few moments for him to register and figure out who I am; then he probably switches to wondering what the hell I'm doing here. "Mr. Douglas. This is an unwelcome surprise."

"If I had a nickel for every time someone said that to me . . ." I walk past him and into the house.

He follows me into the den. "I'm going to have to ask you to leave."

"You can ask, but it's not going to happen."

"Then I will call the police."

"Okay, here's the situation. If you pick up that phone, I will beat you to death with it. Then I will shoot you, which will be an unnecessary act because I would have already beaten you to death. So are we clear? Now sit your ass down on that chair. I have to make a phone call, and then I will tell you exactly what is going to happen."

I take out my cell phone and dial; Stephanie Downes picks up on the third ring. "Mr. Douglas" is how she answers.

"You recognized my ring."

She laughs. "That, and caller ID. To what do I owe this call?"

"You owe it to your being deeply involved in a criminal conspiracy to commit fraud, murder, and a whole bunch of other stuff."

The lightness leaves her voice, which is no great surprise. "What the hell are you talking about?"

"No need to tell you what you already know. But I know everything about the insurance operation; in fact, I owe part of it to you. You never knew Richard Mahler in high school, and his nickname was not Rico."

"We need to talk."

"We're already talking; you need to listen. An hour from now I will be at Jason Musgrove's house with my lawyer. He is prepared to write out a full confession, which we will then deliver to the police and the judge trying my case. You can use the time to get your things together; think of this as a courtesy call."

"Mr. Douglas, I—"

I don't get to hear the end of her sentence because I hang up on her. She doesn't know it, but everything now depends on her.

Five minutes later, Laurie calls me: "She made the call." That is as good a sentence as I've ever heard.

"She may or may not try to leave," I say.

"I'll see that she doesn't."

"Is Marcus in place to clean up if there are any left behind after they leave?"

"Absolutely."

I thank her, hang up, and turn to Jason Musgrove. "Now we wait."

"What are we waiting for?"

"For your close friends to come kill you. Actually, to come kill us."

WHEN Andy arrived at the courthouse, he requested a meeting in chambers with Judge Wallace and Dylan.

Once they were seated, Wallace said, "I must say this is unusual, Mr. Carpenter. My curiosity is piqued."

"*Unusual* is a good way to put it, Your Honor. I didn't want to inform you of this in open court, but my client will not be in court today to hear the verdict."

Dylan made a noise, somewhere between a snort and a grunt, but didn't say any actual words.

"My ears must be deceiving me. Did you just say your client will not be here?"

"I did say that, Your Honor. This is not an issue with your ears."

"Has he violated terms of his bail? Is he missing? Is there a medical emergency?"

"None of the above, Your Honor. There is an emergency, but

it is not medical. It has to do with an investigation Mr. Douglas is conducting, which relates directly to this trial."

"Mr. Carpenter, this is not like cutting a class in high school. His attendance is mandatory."

"I can promise you that if he is found guilty, Mr. Douglas will turn himself in today. But at the risk of further annoying Your Honor, I would point out that his attendance is not mandatory. His absence is unusual, but not illegal. And when this is over, I believe you will consider it justified."

"I will not consider it justified. I want him here within fifteen minutes," Wallace said, his annoyance having turned to anger.

"I'm afraid that is impossible. If Your Honor wants to delay the reading of the verdict, I can guarantee Mr. Douglas's presence tomorrow."

"We will go forward today. Right now."

They all marched into the courtroom. Andy and Eddie Dowd sat alone at the defense table as the jury was brought in. One of Andy's superstitions is that he always puts his hand on his client's shoulder as verdicts are read. The problem in this case was that the client, and his shoulders, were not actually in the courtroom.

"Ladies and gentlemen, have you reached a verdict?"

The foreperson stood and nodded. "Yes, Your Honor. We have."

"YOU know, you should be thanking me."

Jason Musgrove smiles, but he's not really amused. "I should be thanking you?"

I nod. "Yup. They would have killed you for sure. Just like they're going to try to kill you now. You and Stephanie Downes are probably the only two people on the planet who know who they are. They are going to disappear; why would they leave behind loose ends?" I shake my head as if I'm saddened by it all. "After all you did for them, how does it feel to be a loose end?"

He doesn't answer. I go to the window and look out for at least the tenth time. I sure as hell hope they're coming.

Musgrove speaks, the first time in at least a half hour. "Why did you bring your dog?"

"He's not my dog; he's my partner. And unlike your partners, I can trust him. He'll also let me know when they arrive; he is impossible to sneak up on."

As if to prove my point, Simon suddenly sits up, alert. I look out the window and see them pull up, just behind my car. There are two of them; they get out and look around quickly. Determining that nothing is out of the ordinary, they walk to the house.

They don't bother to knock; the door is open. The two of them come in . . . Don Crystal and the man who pretended to be Steven Landry, son of Doris. Steven, or whatever his real name is, is the one holding the gun.

"Well, well . . . I didn't expect you to be here yet," Crystal says to me. "I thought we'd have to kill him and then wait for you."

I frown. "I've got to tell you, you look better in pajamas. Although, the truth is, you look like an asshole either way. In any event, where you're going, they'll tell you how to dress. And you can trade cigarettes for Tang." I then turn to his partner. "Steven, so sorry to hear about your mom."

I'm pretending to be calmer than I am; I wish the bulletproof vest that I'm wearing could cover my entire body and head, but they don't make them like that.

Simon is less interested in acting amiable. He starts to growl.

"Shut that dog up," the fake Steven Landry says.

"Simon. Easy," I say to calm him down. I don't want Landry taking a shot at Simon.

"Hello, Jason," Crystal says, turning to Musgrove with a smile on his face. "Sorry it had to end this way."

"It doesn't," Musgrove says, his voice shaking.

"Oh, but it does. You know far too much."

"My lawyer and partners also know everything," I say. "The jig, to coin a phrase, is up."

Crystal smiles. "Doesn't matter what they know. We will have ceased to exist."

"Amazing," I say. "You create people on a computer, give them full lives, then kill them off and collect the insurance. What a world. And I can barely send an email."

Crystal smiles. "You are indeed in the presence of genius."

"On the other hand, you were too stupid to realize that I used Stephanie Downes to call you and send you here. And you're too stupid to realize that right now there are at least three sets of guns pointed at you."

"Freeze! Drop the weapon!" I think it's Pete Stanton's voice coming from the doorway, but it could be that of Robbie Lillard, standing at the open window.

But Landry does not drop the gun; he raises it to fire. This time I'm certain that it's Pete who centers two bullets on his chest; I watch him do it.

I look at the obviously deceased Landry and shake my head. "I'm just glad his poor mom isn't here to see this."

I watch as Lillard and two officers come in and place Crystal and Musgrove under arrest. I've been calm this entire time, but suddenly my heart starts to pound when I realize that I'm about to find out whether I'm going to prison.

I call Andy on his cell, and he answers with two words.

"Not guilty."

It takes me a little while to reduce the lump in my throat enough to thank him, then I walk over and hug Simon. "Looks like you're stuck with me for a while, buddy."

IT'S been just two days, and already the FBI has completely taken over the investigation.

That is no surprise; the conspiracy has not only crossed state lines, but it probably operated in every state in the country. One of the first things the Feds did was ask to interview me, and I spoke to them for four and a half hours yesterday.

They expected it to be a one-way informational street, but I quickly set different ground rules. In return for providing them with the information I had, and which they desperately needed, I demanded and extracted information from them.

The local mop-up went quickly. Laurie detained Stephanie Downes until the police arrived to place her under arrest. Marcus was at Don Crystal's house, and when he and Landry left, Marcus moved in to detain the two other members of Crystal's cyber team, who were working inside.

Marcus's method of detaining people is slightly different

from Laurie's, but both men had regained consciousness by the time the police arrived. Inside the house was a cyber war room from where the entire conspiracy was implemented and directed.

Downes and the two men, in addition to Don Crystal and Jason Musgrove, have all been indicted for multiple counts of murder and a whole bunch of fraud charges. Federal charges will follow, and I imagine they will supersede most of the local indictments. But the system will handle it, and one way or the other, Crystal and the others are going away for a long time.

According to what I was able to get from the Feds, coupled with what I already knew, the conspiracy was remarkable in its scope and planning. Yet it was also simple in its concept: they created virtual people and then killed them off to collect the insurance. They also created virtual beneficiaries, who were them under different aliases.

Their reach was amazing. Simply by infiltrating and manipulating the cyber world, they gave these fictional people full lives. Some of them were even receiving and cashing Social Security checks. In every respect, they were alive in the cyber world, and the line between that cyber world and the real world has blurred to the point where it doesn't really exist.

Other people like Lisa Yates and Jana Mitchell, working at other companies that are in the same business as Ardmore, were also part of the conspiracy. They were at least partially duped, and while they knew what they were doing was wrong, they didn't realize the scope of what was going on. And they certainly never signed on for murder.

It's been a wild forty-eight hours for me. In addition to answering questions from the FBI and local police, I had to go to court with Andy and do a mea culpa to Judge Wallace. I think down deep he understood my position, but he seemed to think it was his judgely duty to reprimand me and threaten me with contempt of court, before pulling back.

I've also done a lot of media, making the rounds of local stations and cable news outlets. The press has done a lot of digging, and there are estimates that the conspiracy was aiming to bilk a vast array of insurance companies out of between $150 million and $200 million.

Part of the reason that it has become such a big story and will get bigger as more information comes out is that Crystal and his people are showing, to the horror of a nation, that people don't actually have to exist to exist.

Starting tomorrow, Dani, Simon, and I are going to go into relaxation mode. Tonight is the traditional party Andy throws after winning a case. It's at Charlie's, a sports bar that Andy frequents regularly. He says he used to frequent it nightly before he got married.

Andy's whole team is here, and I give a brief toast, thanking them all for their effort, and for my freedom. The entire K Team is here as well, meaning Marcus, Laurie, and Simon. And Dani is here and smiling a lot; she has been through a hell of a lot, just putting up with me.

We have the private upstairs room at Charlie's, and they have agreed to let Simon and Tara attend. Laurie says that Sebastian has chosen to sleep this one out.

We haven't had a chance to talk much, so Laurie and I each grab a beer and sit at a corner table to compare notes. "Leaving the scene when Marcus killed Gardener is still bothering me," she says.

I nod. "I know. But the world is better off with him not in it, and you are better off not having your throat slashed. Marcus did the only thing he could; and you both did the right thing by leaving."

I know she doesn't fully believe that, but maybe she will over time. Andy comes over, his own beer in hand, to join us at the table.

"You're looking pretty serious considering we're at a party," he says.

Laurie nods. "We'll get over it."

"You guys saved my life," I say. "I can't thank—"

Andy cuts me off. "I believe we've beaten this subject to death."

Laurie smiles. "Andy doesn't do well with thank-yous. So on behalf of both of us, you're welcome, Corey. It truly turned out to be our pleasure. Now, I've got some questions for both of you. To start, why did they kill Lisa Yates?"

Andy says, "She must have found out what was going on. She was complicit to a point; Kline recruited her and got her to input information outside the normal procedures. But once she understood the real nature of it, Kline probably threatened her and told her what they were capable of. So she got scared; maybe she was going to go to the authorities; I don't know. But she never got the chance."

"How did you figure it out?" Laurie asks me.

"It was obvious that we were being manipulated; sent in different directions that led to nowhere. And it was all online; they were actually watching Sam trying to watch them. But a key was realizing that the email from Lisa to Doris Landry was faked. There was no Rico; in fact, there was no Doris Landry. Once we found that out, it was just more evidence of their reach and ability to send us into cyber oblivion." I take a sip of my beer before continuing.

"But Steven Landry and his nonexistent mother was the clincher. When she had no emails in her account, and when Sam couldn't connect her to anyone at Somers Point, it was clear she was fabricated. Yet Steven collected on her insurance policy. If they could do it with her, why not on a broad scale?"

"Add to all that the obituary coming out the day before the date on the death certificate. It was a mistake that they made, probably the only one," Andy says.

"And Richard Mahler? Where did he fit in?" Laurie asks.

"Mahler was a patsy; he was set up to take the fall from the beginning, whether we were in the picture or not. Once we became a factor, they led us to the Rico email to shine a light on him. Then Stephanie Downes clinched it with that high school nickname bullshit."

"I believed her and I thought you did also," Laurie says.

"I did, but then I started to think it seemed too convenient. And there was one other thing about her that bugged me. She talked like she and Kline couldn't stand each other and had completely separate client lists. But their assistant told me that they never scheduled seminars at the same time, that they would alternate. It didn't seem to fit."

"So what pointed you toward Crystal?"

"I just realized that this operation had to have begun long before Mahler was hired to replace Crystal. They couldn't take out life insurance policies and then cash them out a few months later; it would be too suspicious. I also didn't buy that he would spend a year in his goddamn pajamas without looking for work.

"One other thing: The first time I met Crystal, he joked about my asking my former buddies in the department to give him a job. But I had never told him that I was an ex-cop. I realized that later."

"And he and his pals were going to ride off into the sunset," Andy says. "They would have had new identities, full new lives created in cyberspace. There would be no connection to their former selves. If the scam was ever discovered, Musgrove would go down for it. He wouldn't even be able to turn on them because he would have no idea what their new identities were."

"Brilliant," Laurie says. "And scary. Nothing is as it seems; no way to tell what is real."

Dani comes over and hears Laurie's comment. "Friends are real. Look around."

Laurie holds up her beer. "I'll drink to that."

Dani turns to me. "So now that you have no GPS bracelet and can go anywhere, what do you want to do tomorrow?"

"How about a barefoot walk in the dirt?"

She shakes her head. "No, I'm too scared of the riptide. How about hanging out at home, just you, me, and Simon?"

Andy says, "Corey, I think she might be a keeper."

"I actually figured that out a while ago."

ACKNOWLEDGMENTS

I haven't done an acknowledgment page for a long time. Basically that is because I live in the world of the famous, and when I mention my celebrated friends, uninformed, bitter people accuse me of being a name-dropper. Well, I'm here to tell you that I am not a name-dropper, and LeBron and Barack would be the first to tell you that.

In any event, that all ends now. I have received tremendous emotional support from many people as I have climbed to the peak of the literary world, and they deserve mention, whether the jealous among us like it or not. So a sincere thank-you to:

Beyoncé; Willie Mays; Willy Loman; Grace and Machine Gun Kelly; Tom Brady; Jan Brady; Marcia Marcia Marcia Brady; the Lee siblings, Bruce, Peggy and Robert E.; Leo DiCaprio; Leo Durocher; Kelley Ragland; Arthur and Sienna Miller; Richard Kimble; Cosmo Kramer; Cosmo Politan; Ben, Paul, and Colonel Hogan; Scott Ryder; Bruno Tattaglia; Vin Scully; My Cousin

Vinny; Robin Rue; Bette, Sammy, and Jefferson Davis; Bradley Cooper; Bill Bradley; Bill Parcells; Elizabeth and Opie Taylor; Madeline Houpt; Jeff Bezos; Jeff Daniels; Stormy Daniels; Beth Miller; D. H. and Jennifer Lawrence; Marie Barone; Latka Gravas; Doug Burns; Ken Burns; Third Degree Burns; Rosalynn and Hurricane Carter; Hillary Strackbein; Alex Trebek; Sylvia Schnauser; Joan Crawford; Rita, Mookie, and Woodrow Wilson; Frank Pentangeli; Debbie Myers; Atticus Finch; Jim and Open Carrey; Eli Manning; and Tom and Tape Delay.

Brandy Allen

DAVID ROSENFELT is the Edgar Award–nominated and Shamus Award–winning author of more than twenty Andy Carpenter novels, most recently *Best in Snow*; nine stand-alone thrillers; two nonfiction titles; and two K Team novels, a new series featuring some of the characters from the Andy Carpenter series. After years of living in California, he and his wife moved to Maine with twenty-five of the four thousand dogs they have rescued.

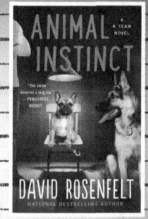
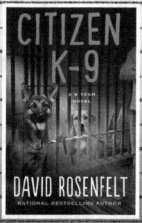

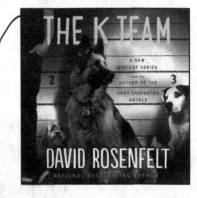